The Mistletoe Murder

The Mistletoe Murder and Other Stories

by the same author

Cover Her Face
A Mind to Murder
Unnatural Causes
Shroud for a Nightingale
An Unsuitable Job for a Woman
The Black Tower
Death of an Expert Witness
Innocent Blood
The Skull beneath the Skin
Devices and Desires
A Taste for Death
The Children of Men
Original Sin
A Certain Justice
Death in Holy Orders
The Murder Room
The Lighthouse
The Private Patient
Death Comes to Pemberley

non-fiction

Time to Be in Earnest:
A Fragment of Autobiography

The Maul and the Pear Tree:
The Ratcliffe Highway Murders 1811
(by P. D. James and T. A. Critchley)

Talking about Detective Fiction

P. D. JAMES

The Mistletoe Murder
and Other Stories

FABER & FABER

This edition first published in the UK in 2016
by Faber & Faber Ltd,
Bloomsbury House,
74–77 Great Russell Street,
London wc1b 3da

Printed in the UK by CPI Group (UK) Ltd, Croydon cro 4yy

Contents

Foreword

Like so many crime writers, P. D. James was drawn to her vocation out of love. Before she took up her pen, she was a keen reader of detective novels, and over her long career she remained fascinated by the so-called Golden Age that followed the end of the First World War. But she was more than a fan. She applied her keen intelligence to what she read and developed a genuine expertise on the subject. I once heard her lecture on the four Queens of Crime – Dorothy L. Sayers, Agatha Christie, Margery Allingham and Ngaio Marsh – and she even wrote a fascinating monograph on the subject, *Talking about Detective Fiction*. That love for the work of her predecessors is evident in this collection of her short stories: she picks the pockets of the mechanics of Golden Age plotting; Agatha Christie is referenced several times; and there are knowing nods to the conventions of traditional 'cosy' mystery stories.

This appropriation of the conventions of the past sometimes misleads people into thinking of P. D. James as a cosy writer. The reality is that she was anything but cosy, and she takes on those conventions only to subvert them in an often witty way. But one thing in particular sets P. D. James apart from the mainstream tradition of Golden Age English crime fiction, with its stately homes and bourgeois villages where reality never rears its ill-mannered head. She understands that murder is nasty and brutal, that it is fuelled by the most malevolent of motives, and she's not afraid to face that darkness head on. Her understanding of what she often called 'wickedness' is creepily accurate. There's nothing cosy about the murders in these stories, however much the settings mimic their forerunners.

And those settings are another hallmark of P. D. James's work. Her stories are always very specifically located in terms both of time and place. She is meticulous in her descriptions, summoning up backdrops against which we can readily picture the events as they unfold. She makes those settings work for a living – they create atmosphere and often foreshadow what is to come. Here is our first sight of Stutleigh Manor: 'It loomed up out of the darkness, a stark shape against a grey sky pierced with a few high stars. And then the moon moved from behind a cloud and the house was revealed; beauty, symmetry and mystery bathed in white light.' We know right now that something sinister and mysterious lies ahead.

As well as wickedness, P. D. James understood the importance of respectability. She wrote about people who would kill to preserve reputation and status, but who would never do it in a vulgar way. Her elegant prose always plays fair with the reader, and lulls us into a sense of false security, as her killers try to do. Behind those untroubled facades, the malice and suspense build, taking us to places that are dark, vicious and shocking. But always beautifully written. These stories are a delicious gift to us at a time when we thought we would read no more of P. D. James's work.

Val McDermid

Preface

Preface

In her introduction to an anthology of short crime stories published in 1934, Dorothy L. Sayers wrote: 'Death seems to provide the minds of the Anglo-Saxon race with a greater fund of innocent amusement than any other single subject.' She was, of course, writing not of the horrifying, messy and occasionally pathetic murders of real life, but of the mysterious, elegantly contrived and popular concoctions of crime writers. Perhaps amusement is hardly the word; entertainment, relaxation or excitement would all be more appropriate. And, to judge from the universal popularity of crime writing, it isn't only the Anglo-Saxons who evince enthusiasm for murder most foul. Millions of readers throughout the world are at home in Sherlock Holmes's claustrophobic sanctum at 221B Baker Street, Miss Marples's charming cottage in St Mary Mead, and Lord Peter Wimsey's elegant Piccadilly flat.

In the period leading up to the Second World War, much of crime writing was done in the form of a short story. The two writers who can be regarded as the founding fathers of the detective story, Edgar Allan Poe and Sir Arthur Conan Doyle, were both masters of the form, and the former adumbrated most of the distinguishing features not only of the short story, but of the crime novel: the least likely suspect as murderer, the closed-room mystery, the case solved by an armchair detective, and the epistolary narrative. Eric Ambler has written: 'The Detective story may have been born in the mind of Edgar Allan Poe, but it was London that fed it, clothed it and brought it to maturity.' He was, of course, thinking of the genius of Conan Doyle, creator of the most famous detective in literature. He bequeathed to the genre a respect for reason, a non-abstract intellectualism, a reliance on ratiocination rather than on physical force, an abhorrence of sentimentality and the power to create an atmosphere of mystery and gothic horror which is yet firmly rooted in physical reality. Above all, more than any other writer he established the tradition of the great detective, that omniscient amateur whose personal, sometimes bizarre eccentricity is contrasted with the rationality of his methods and who provides for the reader the comforting reassurance that, despite our apparent powerlessness, we yet inhabit an intelligible universe.

Although the Sherlock Holmes stories are the most famous of this period, they are not the only ones worth re-reading. Julian Symons, a respected critic of crime fiction, pointed out that most of the notable practitioners in the art of the short story turned to detection as a relief from their other work and enjoyed using a form still in its infancy which offered them infinite opportunities for originality and variation. G. K. Chesterton is an example of a writer whose main interest lay elsewhere but whose Father Brown stories are still read with pleasure. And it is surprising how many other distinguished writers tried their hand at the short crime story. In the second series of *Great Stories of Detection, Mystery and Horror*, published in 1931, the contributors included H. G. Wells, Wilkie Collins, Walter de la Mare, Charles Dickens and Arthur Quiller-Couch, in addition to the names we would expect to find.

Few detective novelists writing today are uninfluenced by the founding fathers, but most crime writers produce novels rather than short stories. Part of the reason for this is the greatly reduced market for short stories generally, but the main reason is perhaps that the detective story has moved closer to mainstream fiction and a writer needs space if he or she is fully to explore the psychological subtleties of character, the complications of relationships, and the impact of murder and of a police investigation on the lives of those characters.

The scope of the short story is inevitably restricted and this means it is most effective when it deals with a single incident or one dominant idea. It is the originality and strength of this idea which largely determine the success of the story. Although it is far less complex in structure than a novel, more linear in concept, driving single-mindedly to its denouement, the short story can still provide within its smaller compass a credible world into which the reader can enter for those satisfactions which we expect from good crime writing: a plausible mystery, tension and excitement, characters with whom we can identify if not always sympathise, and an ending which does not disappoint. There is a satisfying art in containing within a few thousand words all those elements of plot, setting, characterisation and surprise which go to provide a good crime story.

Although most of my own work has been as a novelist, I have greatly enjoyed the challenge of the short story. Much has to be achieved with limited means. There is not space for long and detailed descriptions of place, but the setting must still come alive for the reader. Characterisation is as important as in the novel, but the essentials of a personality must be established with an economy of words. The plot must be strong but not too complex, and the denouement, to which every sentence of the narrative should inexorably lead, must surprise the reader but not leave him feeling cheated. All should command the most ingenious element of the short story: the shock of surprise. The good short story is accordingly difficult to write well, but in this busy age it can provide one of the most satisfactory reading experiences.

P. D. James

The Mistletoe Murder

One of the minor hazards of being a bestselling crime novelist is the ubiquitous question, 'And have you ever been personally involved with a real-life murder investigation?'; a question occasionally asked with a look and tone which suggest that the Murder Squad of the Metropolitan Police might with advantage dig up my back garden.

I invariably reply no, partly from reticence, partly because the truth would take too long to tell and my part in it, even after fifty-two years, is difficult to justify. But now, at seventy, the last survivor of that extraordinary Christmas of 1940, the story can surely safely be told, if only for my own satisfaction. I'll call it 'The Mistletoe Murder'. Mistletoe plays only a small part in the mystery but I've always liked alliteration in my titles. I have changed the names. There is now no one living to be hurt in feelings or reputation, but I don't see why the dead should be denied a similar indulgence.

I was eighteen when it happened, a young war-widow; my husband was killed two weeks after our marriage, one of the first RAF pilots to be shot down in single combat. I had joined the Women's Auxiliary Air Force, partly because I had convinced myself it would have pleased him, but primarily out of the need to assuage grief by a new life, new responsibilities.

It didn't work. Bereavement is like a serious illness. One dies or one survives, and the medicine is time, not a change of scene. I went through my preliminary training in a mood of grim determination to see it through, but when my grandmother's invitation came, just six weeks before Christmas, I accepted with relief. It solved a problem for me. I was an only child and my father, a doctor, had volunteered as a middle-aged recruit to the Royal Army Medical Corps; my mother had taken herself off to America. A number of school friends, some also in the Forces, wrote inviting me for Christmas, but I couldn't face even the subdued festivities of wartime and feared that I should be a skeleton at their family feast.

I was curious, too, about my mother's childhood home. She had never got on with her mother and after her marriage the rift was complete. I had met my grandmother only once in childhood and remembered her as formidable, sharp-tongued, and not particularly sympathetic to the young. But I was no longer young, except in years, and what her letter tactfully hinted at – a warm house with plenty of wood fires, home cooking and good wine, peace and quiet – was just what I craved.

There would be no other guests, but my cousin Paul hoped to be on leave for Christmas. I was curious to

meet him. He was my only surviving cousin, the younger son of my mother's brother and about six years older
than I. We had never met, partly because of the family
feud, partly because his mother was French and much
of his youth spent in that country. His elder brother
had died when I was at school. I had a vague childhood
memory of some disreputable secret, whispered about
but never explained.

My grandmother in her letter assured me that, apart
from the three of us, there would only be the butler,
Seddon, and his wife. She had taken the trouble to find
out the time of a country bus which would leave Victo-
ria at 5 p.m. on Christmas Eve and take me as far as the
nearest town, where Paul would meet me.

The horror of the murder, the concentration on every
hour of that traumatic Boxing Day, has diminished my
memory of the journey and arrival. I recall Christmas
Eve in a series of images, like a gritty black-and-white
film, disjointed, a little surreal.

The bus, blacked out, crawling, lights dimmed,
through the unlit waste of the countryside under a reeling moon; the tall figure of my cousin coming forward
out of the darkness to greet me at the terminus; sitting
beside him, rug-wrapped, in his sports car as we drove
through darkened villages through a sudden swirl of
snow. But one image is clear and magical, my first sight
of Stutleigh Manor. It loomed up out of the darkness, a

stark shape against a grey sky pierced with a few high stars. And then the moon moved from behind a cloud and the house was revealed; beauty, symmetry and mystery bathed in white light.

Five minutes later I followed the small circle of light from Paul's torch through the porch with its country paraphernalia of walking-sticks, brogues, rubber boots and umbrellas, under the blackout curtain and into the warmth and brightness of the square hall. I remember the huge log fire in the hearth, the family portraits, the air of shabby comfort, and the mixed bunches of holly and mistletoe above the pictures and doors, which were the only Christmas decoration. My grandmama came slowly down the wide wooden stairs to greet me, smaller than I had remembered, delicately boned and slightly shorter even than my five feet three inches. But her handshake was surprisingly firm and, looking into the sharp, intelligent eyes, at the set of the obstinate mouth, so like my mother's, I knew that she was still formidable.

I was glad I had come, glad to meet for the first time my only cousin, but my grandmother had in one respect misled me. There was to be a second guest, a distant relation of the family, who had driven from London earlier and arrived before me.

I met Rowland Maybrick for the first time when we gathered for drinks before dinner in a sitting room to the left of the main hall. I disliked him on sight and was grateful to my grandmother for not having suggested that he should drive me from London. The crass insensitivity of his greeting – 'You didn't tell me, Paul, that I was to meet a pretty young widow' – reinforced my initial prejudice against what, with the intolerance of youth, I thought of as a type.

He was in the uniform of a Flight Lieutenant but without wings – Wingless Wonders, we used to call them – darkly handsome, full-mouthed under the thin moustache, his eyes amused and speculative, a man who fancied his chances. I had met his type before and hadn't expected to encounter it at the manor.

I learned that in civilian life he was an antiques dealer. Paul, perhaps sensing my disappointment at finding that I wasn't the only guest, explained that the family needed to sell some valuable coins. Rowland, who specialised in coinage, was to sort and price them with a view to finding a purchaser. And he wasn't only interested in coins. His gaze ranged over furniture, pictures, porcelain and bronze; his long fingers touched and caressed as if he were mentally pricing them for sale. I suspected that, given half a chance, he would have pawed me and assessed my second-hand value.

My grandmother's butler and cook, indispensable small-part characters in any country-house murder, were respectful and competent but deficient in seasonal goodwill. My grandmother, if she gave the matter any thought, would probably have described them as faithful and devoted retainers, but I had my doubts. Even in 1940 things were changing. Mrs Seddon seemed to be both overworked and bored, a depressing combination, while her husband barely contained the lugubrious resentment of a man calculating how much more he could have earned as a war-worker at the nearest RAF base.

I liked my room; the four-poster with its faded curtains, the comfortable low chair beside the fire, the elegant little writing-desk, the prints and watercolours, fly-blown in their original frames. Before getting into bed I put out the bedside light and drew aside the black-out curtain. High stars and moonlight, a dangerous sky. But this was Christmas Eve. Surely they wouldn't fly tonight. And I thought of women all over Europe drawing aside their curtains and looking up in hope and fear at the menacing moon.

I woke early next morning, missing the jangle of Christmas bells, bells which in 1940 would have heralded invasion. Next day the police were to take me through every minute of that Christmas, and every detail remains clearly in my memory more than fifty years later. After breakfast we exchanged presents. My grandmother had obviously raided her jewel chest for her gift to me of a charming enamel and gold brooch, and I suspect that

Paul's offering, a Victorian ring, a garnet surrounded with seed pearls, came from the same source. I had come prepared. I parted with two of my personal treasures in the cause of family reconciliation, a first edition of *A Shropshire Lad* for Paul and an early edition of *Diary of a Nobody* for my grandmother. They were well received. Rowland's contribution to the Christmas rations was three bottles of gin, packets of tea, coffee and sugar, and a pound of butter, probably filched from RAF stores. Just before midday the depleted local church choir arrived, sang half a dozen unaccompanied carols embarrassingly out of tune, were grudgingly rewarded by Mrs Seddon with mulled wine and mince pies and, with evident relief, slipped out again through the blackout curtains to their Christmas dinners.

After a traditional meal served at one o'clock, Paul asked me to go for a walk. I wasn't sure why he wanted my company. He was almost silent as we tramped doggedly over the frozen furrows of desolate fields and through birdless copses as joylessly as if on a route march. The snow had stopped falling but a thin crust lay crisp and white under a gun-metal sky. As the light faded, we returned home and saw the back of the blacked-out manor, a grey L-shape against the whiteness. Suddenly, with an unexpected change of mood, Paul began scooping up the snow. No one receiving the icy slap of a snowball in the face can resist retaliation, and we spent twenty minutes or so like schoolchildren, laughing and hurling snow at each other and at the house, until the snow on the lawn and gravel path had been churned into slush.

The evening was spent in desultory talk in the sitting room, dozing and reading. The supper was light, soup and herb omelettes – a welcome contrast to the heaviness of the goose and Christmas pudding – served very early, as was the custom, so that the Seddons could get away to spend the night with friends in the village. After dinner we moved again to the ground-floor sitting room. Rowland put on the gramophone, then suddenly seized my hands and said, 'Let's dance.' The gramophone was the kind that automatically played a series of records and as one popular disc dropped after another – 'Jeepers Creepers', 'Beer Barrel Polka', 'Tiger Rag', 'Deep Purple' – we waltzed, tangoed, fox-trotted, quick-stepped round the sitting room and out into the hall. Rowland was a superb dancer.

I hadn't danced since Alastair's death but now, caught up in the exuberance of movement and rhythm, I forgot my antagonism and concentrated on following his increasingly complicated lead.

The spell was broken when, breaking into a waltz across the hall and tightening his grasp, he said: 'Our young hero seems a little subdued. Perhaps he's having second thoughts about this job he's volunteered for.'

'What job?'

'Can't you guess? French mother, Sorbonne-educated, speaks French like a native, knows the country. He's a natural.'

I didn't reply. I wondered how he knew, if he had a right to know. He went on:

'There comes a moment when these gallant chaps realise that it isn't play-acting any more. From now on it's for real. Enemy territory beneath you, not dear old Blighty; real Germans, real bullets, real torture-chambers and real pain.'

I thought: And real death, and slipped out of his arms, hearing, as I re-entered the sitting room, his low laugh at my back.

Shortly before ten o'clock my grandmother went up to bed, telling Rowland that she would get the coins out of the study safe and leave them with him. He was due to drive back to London the next day; it would be helpful if he could examine them tonight. He sprang up at once and they left the room together. Her final words to Paul were: 'There's an Edgar Wallace play on the Home Service which I may listen to. It ends at eleven. Come to say goodnight then, if you will, Paul. Don't leave it any later.'

As soon as they'd left, Paul said: 'Let's have the music of the enemy,' and replaced the dance records with Wagner. As I read, he got out a pack of cards from the small desk and played a game of patience, scowling at the cards with furious concentration while the Wagner, much too loud, beat against my ears. When the carriage-clock on the mantelpiece struck eleven, heard in a lull in the music, he swept the cards together and said: 'Time to say goodnight to Grandmama. Is there anything you want?'

'No,' I said, a little surprised. 'Nothing.'

What I did want was the music a little less loud and when he left the room I turned it down. He was back very quickly. When the police questioned me next day, I told them that I estimated that he was away for about three minutes. It certainly couldn't have been longer. He said calmly: 'Grandmama wants to see you.'

We left the sitting room together and crossed the hall. It was then that my senses, preternaturally acute, noticed two facts. One I told the police; the other I didn't. Six mistletoe berries had dropped from the mixed bunch of mistletoe and holly fixed to the lintel above the library door and lay like scattered pearls on the polished floor. And at the foot of the stairs there was a small puddle of water. Seeing my glance, Paul took out his handkerchief and mopped it up. He said: 'I should be able to take a drink up to Grandmama without spilling it.'

She was propped up in bed under the canopy of the four-poster, looking diminished, no longer formidable, but a tired, very old woman. I saw with pleasure that she had been reading the book I'd given her. It lay open on the round bedside table beside the table-lamp, her wireless, the elegant little clock, the small half-full carafe of water with a glass resting over its rim, and a porcelain model of a hand rising from a frilled cuff on which she had placed her rings.

She held out her hand to me; the fingers were limp, the hand cold and listless, the grasp very different from the firm handshake with which she had first greeted me. She said: 'Just to say goodnight, my dear, and thank you for coming. In wartime, family feuds are an indulgence we can no longer afford.'

On impulse I bent down and kissed her forehead. It was moist under my lips. The gesture was a mistake. Whatever it was she wanted from me, it wasn't affection.

We returned to the sitting room. Paul asked me if I drank whisky. When I said that I disliked it, he fetched from the drinks cupboard a bottle for himself and a decanter of claret, then took up the pack of cards again and suggested that he should teach me poker. So that was how I spent Christmas night from about ten past eleven until nearly two in the morning, playing endless games of cards, listening to Wagner and Beethoven, hearing the crackle and hiss of burning logs as I kept up the fire, watching my cousin drink steadily until the whisky bottle was empty. In the end I accepted a glass of claret. It seemed both churlish and censorious to let him drink alone. The carriage-clock struck 1.45 before he roused himself and said: 'Sorry, cousin. Rather drunk. Be glad of your shoulder. To bed, to sleep, perchance to dream.'

We made slow progress up the stairs. I opened his door while he stood propped against the wall. The smell of whisky was only faint on his breath. Then with my help he staggered over to the bed, crashed down and was still.

At eight o'clock next morning Mrs Seddon brought in my tray of early morning tea, switched on the electric fire and went quietly out with an expressionless, 'Good morning, Madam.'

Half-awake, I reached over to pour the first cup when there was a hurried knock, the door opened, and Paul entered. He was already dressed and, to my surprise, showed no signs of a hangover. He said: 'You haven't seen Maybrick this morning, have you?'

'I've only just woken up.'

'Mrs Seddon told me his bed hadn't been slept in. I've just checked. He doesn't appear to be anywhere in the house. And the library door is locked.'

Some of his urgency conveyed itself to me. He held out my dressing-gown and I slipped into it and, after a second's thought, pushed my feet into my outdoor shoes, not my bedroom slippers. I said: 'Where's the library key?'

'On the inside of the library door. We've only the one.'

The hall was dim, even when Paul switched on the light, and the fallen berries from the mistletoe over the library door still gleamed milk-white on the dark wooden floor. I tried the door and, leaning down, looked through the keyhole. Paul was right, the key was in the lock. He said: 'We'll get in through the French windows. We may have to break the glass.'

We went out by a door in the north wing. The air stung my face. The night had been frosty and the thin covering of snow was still crisp except where Paul and I had frolicked the previous day. Outside the library was a small patio about six feet in width leading to a gravel path bordering the lawn. The double set of footprints were plain to see. Someone had entered the library by the French windows and then left by the same route. The footprints were large, a little amorphous, probably made, I thought, by a smooth-soled rubber boot, the first set partly overlaid by the second.

Paul warned: 'Don't disturb the prints. We'll edge our way close to the wall.'

The door in the French windows was closed but not locked. Paul, his back hard against the window, stretched out a hand to open it, slipped inside and drew aside first the blackout curtain and then the heavy brocade.

I followed. The room was dark except for the single green-shaded lamp on the desk. I moved slowly towards it in fascinated disbelief, my heart thudding, hearing behind me a rasp as Paul violently swung back the two sets of curtains. The room was suddenly filled with a clear morning light annihilating the green glow, making horribly visible the thing sprawled over the desk.

He had been killed by a blow of immense force which had crushed the top of his head. Both his arms were stretched out sideways, resting on the desk. His left shoulder sagged as if it, too, had been struck, and the hand was a spiked mess of splintered bones in a pulp of congealed blood. On the desktop the face of his heavy gold wristwatch had been smashed and tiny fragments of glass glittered like diamonds. Some of the coins had rolled onto the carpet and the rest littered the desktop, sent jangling and scattering by the force of the blows. Looking up I checked that the key was indeed in the lock. Paul was peering at the smashed wristwatch.

He said: 'Half-past ten. Either he was killed then or we're meant to believe he was.'

There was a telephone beside the door and I waited, not moving, while he got through to the exchange and called the police. Then he unlocked the door and we went out together. He turned to re-lock – it turned noiselessly as if recently oiled – and pocketed the key. It was then that I noticed that we had squashed some of the fallen mistletoe berries.

Inspector George Blandy arrived within thirty minutes. He was a solidly built countryman, his straw-coloured hair so thick that it looked like thatch above the square, weather-mottled face. He moved with deliberation, whether from habit or because he was still recovering from an over-indulgent Christmas it was impossible to say.

He was followed soon afterwards by the Chief Constable himself. Paul had told me about him. Sir Rouse Armstrong was an ex-colonial Governor, and one of the last of the old school of Chief Constables, obviously past normal retiring age. Very tall, with the face of a meditative eagle, he greeted my grandmother by her Christian name and followed her upstairs to her private sitting room with the grave conspiratorial air of a man called in to advise on some urgent and faintly embarrassing family business. I had the feeling that Inspector Blandy was slightly intimidated by his presence and I hadn't much doubt who would be effectively in charge of this investigation.

I expect you are thinking that this is typical Agatha Christie, and you are right; that's exactly how it struck me at the time. But one forgets, homicide rate excepted, how similar my mother's England was to Dame

Agatha's Mayhem Parva. And it seems entirely appropriate that the body should have been discovered in the library, that most fatal room in popular British fiction.

The body couldn't be moved until the police surgeon arrived. He was at an amateur pantomime in the local town and it took some time to reach him. Dr Bywaters was a rotund, short, self-important little man, red-haired and red-faced, whose natural irascibility would, I thought, have deteriorated into active ill-humour if the crime had been less portentous than murder and the place less prestigious than the manor.

Paul and I were tactfully excluded from the study while he made his examination. Grandmama had decided to remain upstairs in her sitting room. The Seddons, fortified by the consciousness of an unassailable alibi, were occupied making and serving sandwiches and endless cups of coffee and tea, and seemed for the first time to be enjoying themselves. Rowland's Christmas offerings were coming in useful and, to do him justice, I think the knowledge would have amused him. Heavy footsteps tramped backwards and forwards across the hall, cars arrived and departed, telephone calls were made. The police measured, conferred, photographed. The body was eventually taken away shrouded on a stretcher and lifted into a sinister little black van while Paul and I watched from the sitting-room window.

Our fingerprints had been taken, the police explained,

to exclude them from any found on the desk. It was an odd sensation to have my fingers gently held and pressed onto what I remember as a kind of inkpad. We were, of course, questioned, separately and together. I can remember sitting opposite Inspector Blandy, his large frame filling one of the armchairs in the sitting room, his heavy legs planted on the carpet, as conscientiously he went through every detail of Christmas Day. It was only then that I realised that I had spent almost every minute of it in the company of my cousin.

At 7.30 the police were still in the house. Paul invited the Chief Constable to dinner, but he declined, less, I thought, because of any reluctance to break bread with possible suspects, than from a need to return to his grandchildren.

Before leaving he paid a prolonged visit to my grandmother in her room, then returned to the sitting room to report on the results of the day's activities. I wondered whether he would have been as forthcoming if the victim had been a farm labourer and the place the local pub.

He delivered his account with the staccato self-satis-faction of a man confident that he'd done a good day's work.

'I'm not calling in the Yard. I did eight years ago when we had our last murder. Big mistake. All they did was upset the locals. The facts are plain enough. He was killed by a single blow delivered with great force from across the desk and while he was rising from the chair. Weapon, a heavy blunt instrument. The skull was crushed but there was little bleeding – well, you saw for yourselves. I'd say he was a tall murderer; Maybrick was over six foot two. He came through the French windows and went out the same way.

'We can't get much from the footprints, too indistinct, but they're plain enough, the second set overlaying the first. Could have been a casual thief, perhaps a deserter, we've had one or two incidents lately. The blow could have been delivered with a rifle butt. It would be about right for reach and weight. The library door to the garden may have been left open. Your grandmother told her butler Seddon she'd see to the locking up but asked Maybrick to check on the library before he went to bed.

'In the blackout the murderer wouldn't have known the library was occupied. Probably tried the door, went in, caught a gleam of the money and killed almost on impulse.'

Paul asked: 'Then why not steal the coins?'

'Saw that they weren't legal tender. Difficult to get rid of. Or he might have panicked or thought he heard a noise.'

Paul asked: 'And the locked door into the hall?'

'Murderer saw the key and turned it to prevent the

body being discovered before he had a chance to get well away.'

He paused, and his face assumed a look of cunning which sat oddly on the aquiline, somewhat supercilious features. He said: 'An alternative theory is that Maybrick locked himself in. Expected a secret visitor and didn't want to be disturbed. One question I have to ask you, my boy. Rather delicate. How well did you know Maybrick?'

Paul said: 'Only slightly. He's a second cousin.'

'You trusted him? Forgive my asking.'

'We had no reason to distrust him. My grandmother wouldn't have asked him to sell the coins for her if she'd had any doubts. He is family. Distant, but still family.'

'Of course. Family.' He paused, then went on: 'It did occur to me that this could have been a staged attack which went over the top. He could have arranged with an accomplice to steal the coins. We're asking the Yard to look at his London connections.'

I was tempted to say that a faked attack which left the pretend victim with a pulped brain had gone spectacularly over the top, but I remained silent. The Chief Constable could hardly order me out of the sitting room – after all, I had been present at the discovery of the body – but I sensed his disapproval at my obvious interest. A young woman of proper feeling would have followed my grandmother's example and taken to her room.

Paul said: 'Isn't there something odd about that smashed watch? The fatal blow to the head looked so deliberate. But then he strikes again and smashes the hand. Could that have been to establish the exact time of death? If so, why? Or could he have altered the watch before smashing it? Could Maybrick have been killed later?'

The Chief Constable was indulgent to this fancy: 'A bit far-fetched, my boy. I think we've established the time of death pretty accurately. Bywaters puts it at between ten and eleven, judging by the degree of rigor. And we can't be sure in what order the killer struck.

'He could have hit the hand and shoulder first, and then the head. Or he could have gone for the head, then hit out wildly in panic. Pity you didn't hear anything, though.'

Paul said: 'We had the gramophone on pretty loudly and the doors and walls are very solid. And I'm afraid that by 11.30 I wasn't in a state to notice much.'

As Sir Rouse rose to go, Paul asked: 'I'll be glad to have the use of the library if you've finished with it, or do you want to seal the door?'

'No, my boy, that's not necessary. We've done all we need to do. No prints, of course, but then we didn't expect to find them. They'll be on the weapon, no doubt, unless he wore gloves. But he's taken the weapon away with him.'

The house seemed very quiet after the police had left. My grandmother, still in her room, had dinner on a tray and Paul and I, perhaps unwilling to face that empty chair in the dining room, made do with soup and sandwiches in the sitting room. I was restless, physically exhausted; I was also a little frightened.

It would have helped if I could have spoken about the murder, but Paul said wearily: 'Let's give it a rest. We've had enough of death for one day.'

So we sat in silence. From 7.40 we listened to Radio Vaudeville on the Home Service – Billy Cotton and His Band, the BBC Symphony Orchestra with Adrian Boult. After the nine o'clock news and the 9.20 war commentary, Paul murmured that he'd better check with Seddon that he'd locked up.

It was then that, partly on impulse, I made my way across the hall to the library. I turned the door-handle gently as if I feared to see Rowland still sitting at the desk, sorting through the coins with avaricious fingers. The blackout was drawn, the room smelled of old books, not blood. The desk, its top clear, was an ordinary unfrightening piece of furniture, the chair neatly in place.

I stood at the door convinced that this room held a clue to the mystery. Then, from curiosity, I moved over to the desk and pulled out the drawers. On either side was a deep drawer with a shallower one above it. The left was so crammed with papers and files that I had difficulty in opening it. The right-hand deep drawer was clear. I opened the smaller drawer above it. It contained a collection of bills and receipts. Rifling among them I found a receipt for £3,200 from a London coin dealer listing the purchase and dated five weeks previously.

There was nothing else of interest. I closed the drawer and began pacing and measuring the distance from the desk to the French windows. It was then that the door opened almost soundlessly and I saw my cousin.

Coming up quietly beside me, he said lightly: 'What are you doing? Trying to exorcise the horror?'

I replied: 'Something like that.'

For a moment we stood in silence. Then he took my hand in his, drawing it through his arm. He said:

'I'm sorry, cousin, it's been a beastly day for you. And all we wanted was to give you a peaceful Christmas.' I didn't reply. I was aware of his nearness, the warmth of his body, his strength. As we moved together to the door I thought, but did not say: 'Was that really what you wanted, to give me a peaceful Christmas? Was that all?'

I had found it difficult to sleep since my husband had been killed, and now I lay rigid under the canopy of the four-poster reliving the extraordinary day, piecing together the anomalies, the small incidents, the clues, to form a satisfying pattern, trying to impose order on disorder. I think that is what I've been wanting to do all my life. It was that night at Stutleigh which decided my whole career.

Rowland had been killed at half-past ten by a single blow delivered across the width of a three foot six desk. But at half-past ten my cousin had been with me, had indeed been hardly out of my sight all day. I had provided an indisputable alibi. But wasn't that precisely why I had been invited, cajoled to the house by the promise of peace, quiet, good food and wine, exactly what a young widow, recently recruited into the Forces, would yearn for?

The victim, too, had been enticed to Stutleigh. His bait was the prospect of getting his hands on valuable coins and negotiating their sale. But the coins, which I had been told must of necessity be valued and sold, had in fact been purchased only five weeks earlier, almost immediately after my acceptance of my grandmother's invitation. For a moment I wondered why the receipt hadn't been destroyed, but the answer came quickly. The receipt was necessary so that the coins, their purpose now served, could be sold and the £3,200 recouped. And if I had been used, so had other people.

Christmas was the one day when the two servants could be certain to be absent all night. The police, too, could be relied upon to play their appointed part.

The Inspector, honest and conscientious but not

particularly intelligent, inhibited by respect for an old-established family and by the presence of his Chief Constable. The Chief Constable, past retirement age but kept on because of the war, inexperienced in dealing with murder, a friend of the family and the last person to suspect the local squire of a brutal murder.

A pattern was taking shape, was forming into a picture, a picture with a face. In imagination I walked in the footsteps of a murderer. As is proper in a Christie-type crime, I called him X.

Sometime during Christmas Eve the right-hand drawer of the study desk was cleared, the papers stuffed into the left-hand drawer, the wellington boots placed ready. The weapon was hidden, perhaps in the drawer with the boots. No, I reasoned, that wasn't possible; it would need to have been longer than that to reach across the desk. I decided to leave the question of the weapon until later.

And so to the fatal Christmas Day. At a quarter to ten my grandmother goes up to bed, telling Rowland that she will get the coins out of the library safe so that he can examine them before he leaves next day. X can be certain that he will be there at half-past ten, sitting at the desk. He enters silently, taking the key with him and locking the door quietly behind him. The weapon is in his hands, or hidden somewhere within reach in the room.

X kills his victim, smashes the watch to establish the time, exchanges his shoes for the wellington boots, unlocks the door to the patio and opens it wide. Then he takes the longest possible run across the library and leaps into the darkness. He would have to be young, healthy and athletic in order to clear the six feet of snow and land on the gravel path; but then he is young, healthy and athletic.

He need have no fear of footprints on the gravel. The snow has been scuffled by our afternoon snowballing. He makes the first set of footsteps to the library door, closes it, then makes the second set, being careful partly to cover the first. No need to worry about fingerprints on the doorknob; his have every right to be there. And then he re-enters the house by a side-door left unbolted, puts on his own shoes and returns the wellington boots to their place in the front porch. It is while he is crossing the hall that a piece of snow falls from the boots and melts into a puddle on the wooden floor.

How else could that small pool of water have got there? Certainly my cousin had lied in suggesting that it came from the water-carafe. The water-carafe, half-full, had been by my grandmother's bed with the glass over the rim. Water could not have been spilled from it unless the carrier had stumbled and fallen.

And now, at last, I gave the murderer a name. But if my cousin had killed Rowland, how had it been done in

the time? He had left me for no more than three minutes to say goodnight to our grandmother. Could there
have been time to fetch the weapon, go to the library, kill
Rowland, make the footprints, dispose of the weapon,
cleaning from it any blood, and return to me so calmly
to tell me that I was needed upstairs?

But suppose Dr Bywaters was wrong, seduced into
an over-hasty diagnosis by the watch. Suppose Paul had
altered the watch before smashing it and the murder
had taken place later than 10.30. But the medical evidence was surely conclusive; it couldn't have been as late
as half-past one. And even if it were, Paul had been too
drunk to deliver that calculated blow.

But had he in fact been drunk? Had that, too, been a
ploy? He had enquired whether I liked whisky before
bringing in the bottle, and I remembered how faint was
the smell of the spirit on his breath. But no; the timing
was incontrovertible. It was impossible that Paul could
have killed Rowland.

But suppose he'd merely been an accomplice; that
someone else had done the actual deed, perhaps a
fellow-officer whom he had secretly let into the house
and concealed in one of its many rooms, someone who
had stolen down at 10.30 and killed Maybrick while I
gave Paul his alibi and the surging music of Wagner
drowned the sound of the blows. Then, the deed done,
he left the room with the weapon, hiding the key among

the holly and mistletoe above the door, dislodging the bunch as he did so, so that the berries fell. Paul had then come, taking the key from the ledge, being careful to tread over the fallen berries, locked the library door behind him leaving the key in place, then fabricated the footprints just as I'd earlier imagined.

Paul as the accomplice, not the actual murderer, raised a number of unanswered questions, but it was by no means impossible. An Army accomplice would have had the necessary skill and the nerve. Perhaps, I thought bitterly, they'd seen it as a training exercise. By the time I tried to compose myself to sleep I had come to a decision. Tomorrow I would do more thoroughly what the police had done perfunctorily. I would search for the weapon.

Looking back it seems to me that I felt no particular revulsion at the deed and certainly no compulsion to confide in the police. It wasn't just that I liked my cousin and had disliked Maybrick. I think the war had something to do with it. Good people were dying all over the world and the fact that one unlikeable one had been killed seemed somehow less important.

I know now that I was wrong. Murder should never be excused or condoned. But I don't regret what I later did; no human being should die at the end of a rope.

I woke very early before it was light. I possessed myself in patience; there was no use in searching by artificial light and I didn't want to draw attention to myself. So I waited until Mrs Seddon had brought up my early morning tea, bathed and dressed, and went down to breakfast just before nine. My cousin wasn't there. Mrs Seddon said that he had driven to the village to get the car serviced. This was the opportunity I needed.

My investigation ended in a small lumber room at the top of the house. It was so full that I had to climb over trunks, tin boxes and old chests in order to search. There was a wooden chest containing rather battered cricket bats and balls, dusty, obviously unused since the grandsons last played in village matches. I touched a magnificent but shabby-looking horse, and set it in vigorous creaking motion, got tangled in the piled tin track of a Hornby train set, and cracked my ankle against a large Noah's Ark.

Under the single window was a long wooden box, which I opened. Dust rose from a sheet of brown paper covering six croquet mallets with balls and hoops. It struck me that a mallet, with its long handle, would have been an appropriate weapon, but these had clearly lain undisturbed for years. I replaced the lid and searched further.

In a corner were two golf-bags, and it was here I found what I was looking for – one of the clubs, the kind with a large wooden head, was different from its fellows. The head was shining-clean.

It was then I heard a footstep and, looking round, saw my cousin. I know that guilt must have been plain on my face but he seemed completely unworried.

He asked: 'Can I help you?'

No,' I said. 'No. I was just looking for something.'

'And have you found it?'

'Yes,' I said. 'I think I have.' He came into the room and shut the door, leaned across it and said casually: 'Did you like Rowland Maybrick?'

'No,' I said. 'No, I didn't like him. But not liking him isn't a reason for killing him.'

He said easily: 'No, it isn't, is it? But there's something I think you should know about him. He was responsible for the death of my elder brother.'

'You mean he murdered him?'

'Nothing as straightforward as that. He blackmailed him. Charles was a homosexual. Maybrick got to know and made him pay. Charles killed himself because he couldn't face a life of deceit, of being in Maybrick's power, of losing this place. He preferred the dignity of death.'

Looking back on it I have to remind myself how different public attitudes were in the Forties. Now it would seem extraordinary that anyone would kill himself for such a motive. Then I knew with desolate certainty that what he said was true.

I asked: 'Does my grandmother know about the homosexuality?'

'Oh yes. There isn't much that her generation don't know, or guess. Grandmama adored Charles.'

'I see. Thank you for telling me.' After a moment I said: 'I suppose if you'd gone on your first mission knowing Rowland Maybrick was alive and well, you'd have felt there was unfinished business.'

He said: 'How clever you are, Cousin. And how well you put things. That's exactly what I should have felt, that I'd left unfinished business.' Then he added: 'So what were you doing here?'

I took out my handkerchief and looked him in the face, the face so disconcertingly like my own.

I said: 'I was just dusting the tops of the golf-clubs.'

I left the house two days later. We never spoke of it again. The investigation continued its fruitless course. I could have asked my cousin how he had done it, but I didn't. For years I thought I should never really know.

My cousin died in France, not, thank God, under Gestapo interrogation, but shot in an ambush. I wondered whether his Army accomplice had survived the war or had died with him. My grandmother lived on alone in the house, not dying until she was ninety-one, when she left the property to a charity for indigent gentlewomen, either to maintain as a home or to sell. It was the last charity I would have expected her to choose. The charity sold.

My grandmother's one bequest to me was the books

in the library. Most of these I, too, sold, but I went down to the house to look them over and decide which volumes I wished to keep. Among them I found a photograph album wedged between two rather dull tomes of nineteenth-century sermons. I sat at the same desk where Rowland had been murdered and turned the pages, smiling at the sepia photographs of high-bosomed ladies with their clinched waists and immense flowered hats.

And then, suddenly, turning its stiff pages, I saw my grandmother as a young woman. She was wearing what seemed a ridiculous little cap like a jockey's and holding a golf-club as confidently as if it were a parasol. Beside the photograph was her name in careful script and underneath was written: 'Ladies County Golf Champion 1898'.

A Very Commonplace Murder

'We close at twelve on Saturday,' said the blonde in the estate office. 'So if you keep the key after then, please drop it back through the letterbox. It's the only key we have, and there may be other people wanting to view on Monday. Sign here, please, Sir.'

The 'Sir' was grudging, an afterthought. Her tone was reproving. She didn't really think he would buy the flat, this seedy old man with his air of spurious gentility, with his harsh voice. In her job you soon got a nose for the genuine inquirer. Ernest Gabriel. An odd name, half-common, half-fancy.

But he took the key politely enough and thanked her for her trouble. No trouble, she thought. God knew there were few enough people interested in that sordid little dump, not at the price they were asking. He could keep the key a week, for all she cared.

She was right. Gabriel hadn't come to buy, only to view. It was the first time he had been back since it all happened sixteen years ago. He came neither as a pilgrim nor a penitent. He had returned under some compulsion which he hadn't even bothered to analyse. He had been on his way to visit his only living relative, an elderly aunt who had recently been admitted to a geriatric ward. He hadn't even realised the bus would pass the flat.

But suddenly they were lurching through Camden Town, and the road became familiar, like a photograph springing into focus; and with a frisson of surprise he recognised the double-fronted shop and the flat above. There was an estate agent's notice in the window. Almost without thinking, he had got off at the next stop, gone back to verify the name, and walked the half-mile to the office. It had seemed as natural and inevitable as his daily bus journey to work.

Twenty minutes later he fitted the key into the lock of the front door and passed into the stuffy emptiness of the flat. The grimy walls still held the smell of cooking. There was a spatter of envelopes on the worn linoleum, dirtied and trampled by the feet of previous viewers. The light bulb swung naked in the hall, and the door into the sitting room stood open. To his right was the staircase, to his left the kitchen.

Gabriel paused for a moment, then went into the kitchen. From the windows, half-curtained with grubby gingham, he looked upward to the great black building facing the flat, eyeless except for the one small square of window high on the fifth floor. It was from this window, sixteen years ago, that he had watched Denis Speller and Eileen Morrisey play out their commonplace little tragedy to its end.

He had no right to be watching them, no right to be in the building at all after six o'clock. That had been the nub of his awful dilemma. It had happened by chance. Mr Maurice Bootman had instructed him, as the firm's filing clerk, to go through the papers in the late Mr Bootman's upstairs den in case there were any which should be in the files. They weren't confidential or important papers – those had been dealt with by the family and the firm's solicitors months before. They were just a miscellaneous, yellowing collection of out-of-date memoranda, old accounts, receipts and fading press clippings which had been bundled together into old Mr Bootman's desk. He had been a great hoarder of trivia.

But at the back of the left-hand bottom drawer Gabriel had found a key. It was by chance that he tried it in the lock of the corner cupboard. It fitted. And in the cupboard Gabriel found the late Mr Bootman's small but choice collection of pornography.

He knew that he had to read the books; not just to snatch surreptitious minutes with one ear listening for a footstep on the stairs or the whine of the approaching lift, and fearful always that his absence from his filing room would be noticed. No, he had to read them in privacy and in peace. So he devised his plan.

It wasn't difficult. As a trusted member of the staff, he had one of the Yale keys to the side-door at which goods were delivered. It was locked on the inside at night by the porter before he went off duty. It wasn't hard for Gabriel, always among the last to go home, to find the opportunity of shooting back the bolts before leaving with the porter by the main door. He dared risk it only once a week, and the day he chose was Friday.

He would hurry home, eat his solitary meal beside the gas fire in his bedsitting room, then make his way back to the building and let himself in by the side-door. All that was necessary was to make sure he was waiting for the office to open on Monday morning so that, among the first in, he could lock the side-door before the porter made his ritual visit to unlock it for the day's deliveries.

These Friday nights became a desperate but shameful joy to Gabriel. Their pattern was always the same. He would sit crouched in old Mr Bootman's low leather chair in front of the fireplace, his shoulders hunched over the book in his lap, his eyes following the pool of light from his torch as it moved over each page. He never dared to switch on the room light, and even on the coldest night he never lit the gas fire. He was fearful that its hiss might mask the sound of approaching feet, that its glow might shine through the thick curtains at the window, or that, somehow, the smell of gas would linger in the room next Monday morning to betray him. He was morbidly afraid of discovery, yet even this fear added to the excitement of his secret pleasure.

It was on the third Friday in January that he first saw them. It was a mild evening, but heavy and starless. An early rain had slimed the pavements and bled the scribbled headlines from the newspaper placards. Gabriel wiped his feet carefully before climbing to the fifth floor. The claustrophobic room smelled sour and dusty, the air struck colder than the night outside. He wondered whether he dared open the window and let in some of the sweetness of the rain-cleansed sky.

It was then that he saw the woman. Below him were the back entrances of the two shops, each with a flat above. One flat had boarded windows, but the other looked lived in. It was approached by a flight of iron steps leading to an asphalt yard. He saw the woman in the glow of a street lamp as she paused at the foot of the steps, fumbling in her handbag. Then, as if gaining resolution, she came swiftly up the steps and almost ran across the asphalt to the flat door.

He watched as she pressed herself into the shadow of the doorway, then swiftly turned the key in the lock and slid out of his sight. He had time only to notice that she was wearing a pale mackintosh buttoned high under a mane of fairish hair and that she carried a string bag of what looked like groceries. It seemed an oddly furtive and solitary homecoming.

Gabriel waited. Almost immediately he saw the light go on in the room to the left of the door. Perhaps she was in the kitchen. He could see her faint shadow passing to and fro, bending and then lengthening. He guessed that she was unpacking the groceries. Then the light in the room went out.

For a few moments the flat was in darkness. Then the light in the upstairs window went on, brighter this time, so that he could see the woman more plainly. She could not know how plainly. The curtains were drawn, but they were thin. Perhaps the owners, confident that they were not overlooked, had grown careless. Although the woman's silhouette was only a faint blur, Gabriel could see that she was carrying a tray. Perhaps she was intending to eat her supper in bed. She was undressing now.

He could see her lifting the garments over her head and twisting down to release stockings and take off her shoes. Suddenly she came very close to the window, and he saw the outline of her body plainly. She seemed to be watching and listening. Gabriel found that he was holding his breath. Then she moved away, and the light dimmed. He guessed that she had switched off the central bulb and was using the bedside lamp. The room was now lit with a softer, pinkish glow within which the woman moved, insubstantial as a dream.

Gabriel stood with his face pressed against the cold window, still watching. Shortly after eight o'clock the boy arrived. Gabriel always thought of him as 'the boy'. Even from that distance his youth, his vulnerability, were apparent. He approached the flat with more confidence than the woman, but still swiftly, pausing at the top of the steps as if to assess the width of the rain-washed yard.

She must have been waiting for his knock. She let him in at once, the door barely opening. Gabriel knew that she had come naked to let him in. And then there were two shadows in the upstairs room, shadows that met and parted and came together again before they moved, joined, to the bed and out of Gabriel's sight.

The next Friday he watched to see if they would come again. They did, and at the same times, the woman first, at twenty minutes past seven, the boy forty minutes later. Again Gabriel stood, rigidly intent at his watching post, as the light in the upstairs window sprang on and then was lowered. The two naked figures, seen dimly behind the curtains, moved to and fro, joined and parted, fused and swayed together in a ritualistic parody of a dance.

This Friday, Gabriel waited until they left. The boy came out first, sidling quickly from the half-open door and almost leaping down the steps, as if in exultant joy. The woman followed five minutes later, locking the door behind her and darting across the asphalt, her head bent.

After that he watched for them every Friday. They

held a fascination for him even greater than Mr Bootman's books. Their routine hardly varied. Sometimes
the boy arrived a little late, and Gabriel would see the
woman watching motionless for him behind the bedroom curtains. He too would stand with held breath,
sharing her agony of impatience, willing the boy to
come. Usually the boy carried a bottle under his arm,
but one week it was in a wine basket, and he bore it
with great care. Perhaps it was an anniversary, a special
evening for them. Always the woman had the bag of
groceries. Always they ate together in the bedroom.

Friday after Friday, Gabriel stood in the darkness,
his eyes fixed on that upstairs window, straining to deci-
pher the outlines of their naked bodies, picturing what
they were doing to each other.

They had been meeting for seven weeks when it happened. Gabriel was late at the building that night. His
usual bus did not run, and the first to arrive was full.
By the time he reached his watching-post, there was
already a light in the bedroom. He pressed his face to
the window, his hot breath smearing the pane. Hastily rubbing it clear with the cuff of his coat, he looked
again. For a moment he thought that there were two
figures in the bedroom. But that must surely be a freak
of the light. The boy wasn't due for thirty minutes yet.
But the woman, as always, was on time.

Twenty minutes later he went into the bathroom on

the floor below. He had become much more confident during the last few weeks and now moved about the building, silently, and using only his torch for light, but with almost as much assurance as during the day. He spent nearly ten minutes in the bathroom. His watch showed that it was just after eight by the time he was back at the window, and, at first, he thought that he had missed the boy. But no, the slight figure was even now running up the steps and across the asphalt to the shelter of the doorway.

Gabriel watched as he knocked and waited for the door to open. But it didn't open. She didn't come. There was a light in the bedroom, but no shadow moved on the curtains. The boy knocked again. Gabriel could just detect the quivering of his knuckles against the door. Again he waited. Then the boy drew back and looked up at the lighted window. Perhaps he was risking a low-pitched call. Gabriel could hear nothing, but he could sense the tension in that waiting figure.

Again the boy knocked. Again there was no response. Gabriel watched and suffered with him until, at twenty past eight, the boy finally gave up and turned away. Then Gabriel too stretched his cramped limbs and made his way into the night. The wind was rising, and a young moon reeled through the torn clouds. It was getting colder. He wore no coat and missed its comfort. Hunching his shoulders against the bite of the wind, he knew that this was the last Friday he would come late to the building. For him, as for that desolate boy, it was the end of a chapter.

He first read about the murder in his morning paper on his way to work the following Monday. He recognised the picture of the flat at once, although it looked oddly unfamiliar with the bunch of plainclothes detectives conferring at the door and the stolid uniformed policeman at the top of the steps.

The story so far was slight. A Mrs Eileen Morrisey, aged thirty-four, had been found stabbed to death in a flat in Camden Town late on Sunday night. The discovery was made by the tenants, Mr and Mrs Kealy, who had returned late on Sunday from a visit to Mr Kealy's parents. The dead woman, who was the mother of twin daughters aged twelve, was a friend of Mrs Kealy. Detective Chief Inspector William Holbrook was in charge of the investigation. It was understood that the dead woman had been sexually assaulted.

Gabriel folded his paper with the same precise care as he did on any ordinary day. Of course, he would have to tell the police what he had seen. He couldn't let an innocent man suffer, no matter what the inconvenience to himself. The knowledge of his intention, of his public-spirited devotion to justice, was warmly satisfying. For the rest of the day he crept around his filing cabinets with the secret complacency of a man dedicated to sacrifice.

But somehow his first plan of calling at a police station on his way home from work came to nothing. There was no point in acting hastily. If the boy were arrested, he would speak. But it would be ridiculous to prejudice his reputation and endanger his job before he even knew whether the boy was a suspect. The police might never learn of the boy's existence. To speak up now might only focus suspicion on the innocent. A prudent man would wait. Gabriel decided to be prudent.

The boy was arrested three days later. Again Gabriel read about it in his morning paper. There was no picture this time, and few details. The news had to compete with a society elopement and a major air crash and did not make the first page. The inch of newsprint stated briefly: 'Denis John Speller, a butcher's assistant, aged nineteen, who gave an address at Muswell Hill, was today charged with the murder of Mrs Eileen Morrisey, the mother of twelve-year-old twins, who was stabbed to death last Friday in a flat in Camden Town.'

So the police now knew more precisely the time of death. Perhaps it was time for him to see them. But how could he be sure that this Denis Speller was the young lover he had been watching these past Friday nights? A woman like that – well, she might have had any number of men. No photograph of the accused would be published in any paper until after the trial. But more information would come out at the preliminary hearing. He would wait for that. After all, the accused might not even be committed for trial.

Besides, he had himself to consider. There had been time to think of his own position. If young Speller's life were in danger, then, of course, Gabriel would tell what he had seen. But it would mean the end of his job with Bootman's. Worse, he would never get another. Mr Maurice Bootman would see to that. He, Gabriel, would be branded as a dirty-minded, sneaking little voyeur, a Peeping Tom who was willing to jeopardise his livelihood for an hour or two with a naughty book and a chance to pry into other people's happiness. Mr Maurice would be too angry at the publicity to forgive the man who had caused it.

And the rest of the firm would laugh. It would be the best joke in years, funny and pathetic and futile. The pedantic, respectable, censorious Ernest Gabriel found out at last! And they wouldn't even give him credit for speaking up. It simply wouldn't occur to them that he could have kept silent.

If only he could think of a good reason for being in the building that night. But there was none. He could hardly say that he had stayed behind to work late, when he had taken such care to leave with the porter. And it wouldn't do to say that he had returned later to catch up with his filing. His filing was always up to date, as he was fond of pointing out. His very efficiency was against him.

Besides, he was a poor liar. The police wouldn't accept his story without probing. After they had spent so much time on the case, they would hardly welcome his tardy revelation of new evidence. He pictured the circle of grim, accusing faces, the official civility barely concealing their dislike and contempt. There was no sense in inviting such an ordeal before he was sure of the facts.

But after the preliminary hearing, at which Denis Speller was sent up for trial, the same arguments seemed equally valid. By now he knew that Speller was the lover he had seen. There had never really been much room for doubt. By now, too, the outlines of the case for the Crown were apparent. The prosecution would seek to prove that this was a crime of passion, that the boy, tormented by her threat to leave him, had killed in jealousy or revenge. The accused would deny that he had entered the flat that night, would state again and again that he had knocked and gone away. Only Gabriel could support his story. But it would still be premature to speak.

He decided to attend the trial. In that way he would hear the strength of the Crown's case. If it appeared likely that the verdict would be 'Not Guilty', he could remain silent. And if things went badly, there was an excitement, a fearful fascination, in the thought of rising to his feet in the silence of that crowded court and speaking out his evidence before all the world. The questioning, the criticism, the notoriety would have come later. But he would have had his moment of glory.

He was surprised and a little disappointed by the court. He had expected a more imposing, more dramatic setting for justice than this modern, clean-smelling, businesslike room. Everything was quiet and orderly. There was no crowd at the door jostling for seats. It wasn't even a popular trial.

Sliding into his seat at the back of the court, Gabriel looked round, at first apprehensively and then with more confidence. But he needn't have worried. There was no one there he knew. It was really a very dull collection of people, hardly worthy, he thought, of the drama that was to be played out before them. Some of them looked as if they might have worked with Speller or lived in the same street. All looked ill at ease, with the slightly shifty air of people who find themselves in unusual or intimidating surroundings. There was a thin woman in black crying softly into a handkerchief. No one took any notice of her; no one comforted her.

From time to time one of the doors at the back of the court would open silently, and a newcomer would sidle almost furtively into his seat. When this happened, the row of faces would turn momentarily to him without interest, without recognition, before turning their eyes again to the slight figure in the dock.

Gabriel stared too. At first he dared to cast only fleeting glances, averting his eyes suddenly, as if each glance were a desperate risk. It was unthinkable that the prisoner's eyes should meet his, should somehow know that here was the man who could save him and should signal a desperate appeal. But when he had risked two or three glances, he realised there was nothing to fear. That solitary figure was seeing no one, caring about no one except himself. He was only a bewildered and terrified boy, his eyes turned inward to some private hell. He looked like a trapped animal, beyond hope and beyond fight.

The judge was rotund, red-faced, his chins sunk into the bands at his neck. He had small hands, which he rested on the desk before him except when he was making notes. Then counsel would stop talking for a moment before continuing more slowly, as if anxious not to hurry his Lordship, watching him like a worried father explaining with slow deliberation to a not very bright child.

But Gabriel knew where lay the power. The judge's chubby hands, folded on the desk like a parody of a child in prayer, held a man's life in their grasp. There was only one person in the court with more power than that scarlet-sashed figure high under the carved coat of arms. And that was he, Gabriel. The realisation came to him in a spurt of exultation, at once intoxicating and satisfying. He hugged his knowledge to himself gloatingly. This was a new sensation, terrifyingly sweet.

He looked round at the solemn watching faces and wondered how they would change if he got suddenly to his feet and called out what he knew. He would say it firmly, confidently. They wouldn't be able to frighten him. He would say, 'My Lord. The accused is innocent. He did knock and go away. I, Gabriel, saw him.'

And then what would happen? It was impossible to guess. Would the judge stop the trial so that they could all adjourn to his chambers and hear his evidence in private? Or would Gabriel be called now to take his stand in the witness box? One thing was certain – there would be no fuss, no hysteria.

But suppose the judge merely ordered him out of the court. Suppose he was too surprised to take in what Gabriel had said. Gabriel could picture him leaning forward irritably, hand to his ear, while the police at the back of the court advanced silently to drag out the offender. Surely in this calm, aseptic atmosphere, where justice itself seemed an academic ritual, the voice of truth would be merely a vulgar intrusion. No one would believe him. No one would listen. They had set this elaborate scene to play out their drama to the end.

They wouldn't thank him for spoiling it now. The time to speak had passed.

Even if they did believe him, he wouldn't get any credit now for coming forward. He would be blamed for leaving it so late, for letting an innocent man get so close to the gallows. If Speller were innocent, of course. And who could tell that? They would say that he might have knocked and gone away, only to return later and gain access to kill. He, Gabriel, hadn't waited at the window to see. So his sacrifice would have been for nothing.

And he could hear those taunting office voices: 'Trust old Gabriel to leave it to the last minute. Bloody coward. Read any naughty books lately, Archangel?' He would be sacked from Bootman's without even the consolation of standing well in the public eye.

Oh, he would make the headlines, all right. He could imagine them: *Outburst in Old Bailey. Man Upholds Accused's Alibi*. Only it wasn't an alibi. What did it really prove? He would be regarded as a public nuisance, the pathetic little voyeur who was too much of a coward to go to the police earlier. And Denis Speller would still hang.

Once the moment of temptation had passed and he knew with absolute certainty that he wasn't going to speak, Gabriel began almost to enjoy himself. After all, it wasn't every day that one could watch British justice at work. He listened, noted, appreciated. It was a formidable case which the prosecution unfolded. Gabriel approved of the prosecuting counsel. With his high forehead, beaked nose, and bony, intelligent face, he looked so much more distinguished than the judge. This was how a famous lawyer should look. He made his case without passion, almost without interest. But that, Gabriel knew, was how the law worked. It wasn't the duty of prosecuting counsel to work for a conviction. His job was to state with fairness and accuracy the case for the Crown.

He called his witnesses. Mrs Brenda Kealy, the wife of the tenant of the flat. A blonde, smartly dressed, common little slut if ever Gabriel saw one. Oh, he knew her type, all right. He could guess what his mother would have said about her. Anyone could see what she was interested in. And by the look of her, she was getting it regularly, too. Dressed up for a wedding. A tart if ever he saw one.

Snivelling into her handkerchief and answering counsel's questions in a voice so low that the judge had to ask her to speak up. Yes, she had agreed to lend Eileen the flat on Friday nights. She and her husband went every Friday to visit his parents at Southend. They always left as soon as he shut the shop. No, her husband didn't know of the arrangement. She had given Mrs Morrisey the spare key without consulting him. There wasn't any other spare key that she knew of.

Why had she done it? She was sorry for Eileen. Eileen had pressed her. She didn't think the Morriseys had much of a life together.

Here the judge interposed gently that the witness should confine herself to answering counsel's questions. She turned to him. 'I was only trying to help Eileen, my Lord.'

Then there was the letter. It was passed to the snivelling woman in the box, and she confirmed that it had been written to her by Mrs Morrisey. Slowly it was collected by the clerk and borne majestically across to counsel, who proceeded to read it aloud:

Dear Brenda,

We shall be at the flat on Friday after all. I thought I'd better let you know in case you and Ted changed your plans. But it will definitely be for the last time. George is getting suspicious, and I must think of the children. I always knew it would have to end. Thank you for being such a pal.

Eileen

The measured, upper-class voice ceased. Looking across at the jury, counsel laid the letter slowly down. The judge bent his head and made another notation. There was a moment of silence in the court. Then the witness was dismissed.

And so it went on. There was the paper-seller at the end of Moulton Street who remembered Speller buying an *Evening Standard* just before eight o'clock. The accused was carrying a bottle under his arm and seemed very cheerful. He had no doubt his customer was the accused.

There was the publican's wife from the Rising Sun at the junction of Moulton Mews and High Street who testified that she served the prisoner with a whisky shortly before half-past eight. He hadn't stayed long. Just long enough to drink it down. He had seemed very upset. Yes, she was quite sure it was the accused. There was a motley collection of customers to confirm her evidence. Gabriel wondered why the prosecution had bothered to call them, until he realised that Speller had denied visiting the Rising Sun, had denied that he had needed a drink.

There was George Edward Morrisey, described as an estate agent's clerk, thin-faced, tight-lipped, standing rigidly in his best blue serge suit. He testified that his marriage had been happy, that he had known nothing, suspected nothing. His wife had told him that she spent Friday evenings learning to make pottery at evening classes. The court tittered. The judge frowned.

In reply to counsel's questions, Morrisey said that he had stayed at home to look after the children. They were still a little young to be left alone at night. Yes, he had been at home the night his wife was killed. Her death was a great grief to him. Her liaison with the accused had come as a terrible shock. He spoke the word 'liaison' with an angry contempt, as if it were bitter on his tongue. Never once did he look at the prisoner.

There was the medical evidence – sordid, specific but mercifully clinical and brief. The deceased had been raped, then stabbed three times through the jugular vein. There was the evidence of the accused's employer, who contributed a vague and imperfectly substantiated story about a missing meat-screwer. There was the prisoner's landlady, who testified that he had arrived home on the night of the murder in a distressed state and that he had not got up to go to work next morning. Some of the threads were thin. Some, like the evidence of the butcher, obviously bore little weight even in the eyes of the prosecution. But together they were weaving a rope strong enough to hang a man.

The defending counsel did his best, but he had the desperate air of a man who knows that he is foredoomed to lose. He called witnesses to testify that Speller was a gentle, kindly boy, a generous friend, a good son and brother. The jury believed them. They also believed that he had killed his mistress. He called the accused. Speller was a poor witness, unconvincing, inarticulate. It would have helped, thought Gabriel, if the boy had shown some sign of pity for the dead woman. But he was too absorbed in his own danger to spare a thought for anyone else. Perfect fear casteth out love, thought Gabriel. The aphorism pleased him.

The judge summed up with scrupulous impartiality, treating the jury to an exposition on the nature and value of circumstantial evidence and an interpretation of the expression 'reasonable doubt'. The jury listened with respectful attention. It was impossible to guess what went on behind those twelve pairs of watchful, anonymous eyes. But they weren't out long.

Within forty minutes of the court rising, they were back; the prisoner reappeared in the dock, the judge asked the formal question. The foreman gave the expected answer, loud and clear. 'Guilty, my Lord.' No one seemed surprised.

The judge explained to the prisoner that he had been found guilty of the horrible and merciless killing of the woman who had loved him. The prisoner, his face taut and ashen, stared wild-eyed at the judge, as if only half-hearing. The sentence was pronounced, sounding doubly horrible spoken in those soft judicial tones.

Gabriel looked with interest for the black cap and saw with surprise and some disappointment that it was merely a square of some black material perched incongruously atop the judge's wig. The jury was thanked. The judge collected his notes like a businessman clearing his desk at the end of a busy day. The court rose. The prisoner was taken below. It was over.

The trial caused little comment at the office. No one knew that Gabriel had attended. His day's leave 'for personal reasons' was accepted with as little interest as any previous absence. He was too solitary, too unpopular to be included in office gossip. In his dusty and ill-lit room, insulated by tiers of filing cabinets, he was the object of vague dislike or, at best, of a pitying tolerance. The filing room had never been a centre for cosy office chat. But he did hear the opinion of one member of the firm.

On the day after the trial, Mr Bootman, newspaper in hand, came into the general office while Gabriel was distributing the morning mail. 'I see they've disposed of our little local trouble,' Mr Bootman said. 'Apparently the fellow is to hang. A good thing, too. It seems to have been the usual sordid story of illicit passion and general stupidity. A very commonplace murder.'

No one replied. The office staff stood silent, then stirred into life. Perhaps they felt that there was nothing more to be said.

It was shortly after the trial that Gabriel began to dream. The dream, which occurred about three times a week, was always the same. He was struggling across a desert under a blood-red sun, trying to reach a distant fort. He could sometimes see the fort clearly, although it never got any closer. There was an inner courtyard crowded with people, a silent black-clad multitude whose faces were all turned towards a central platform. On the platform was a gallows. It was a curiously elegant structure, with two sturdy posts at either side and a delicately curved crosspiece from which the noose dangled.

The people, like the gallows, were not of this age. It was a Victorian crowd, the women in shawls and bonnets, the men in top hats or narrow-brimmed bowlers. He could see his mother there, her thin face peaked under the widow's veil. Suddenly she began to cry, and as she cried, her face changed and became the face of the weeping woman at the trial. Gabriel longed desperately to reach her, to comfort her. But with every step he sank deeper into the sand.

There were people on the platform now. One, he knew, must be the prison governor, top-hatted, frock-coated, bewhiskered and grave. His clothes were those of a Victorian gentleman, but his face, under that luxuriant beard, was the face of Mr Bootman. Beside him stood the chaplain, in gown and bands, and, on either side, were two warders, their dark jackets buttoned high to their necks.

Under the noose stood the prisoner. He was wearing breeches and an open-necked shirt, and his neck was as white and delicate as a woman's. It might have been that other neck, so slender it looked. The prisoner was gazing across the desert towards Gabriel, not with desperate appeal but with great sadness in his eyes. And, this time, Gabriel knew that he had to save him, had to get there in time.

But the sand dragged at his aching ankles, and although he called that he was coming, coming, the wind, like a furnace blast, tore the words from his parched throat. His back, bent almost double, was blistered by the sun. He wasn't wearing a coat. Somehow, irrationally, he was worried that his coat was missing, that something had happened to it that he ought to remember.

As he lurched forward, floundering through the gritty morass, he could see the fort shimmering in the heat haze. Then it began to recede, getting fainter and further, until at last it was only a blur among the distant sandhills. He heard a high, despairing scream from the courtyard – then awoke to know that it was his voice and that the damp heat on his brow was sweat, not blood.

In the comparative sanity of the morning, he analysed the dream and realised that the scene was one pictured in a Victorian news-sheet which he had once seen in the window of an antiquarian bookshop. As he remembered, it showed the execution of William Corder for the murder of Maria Marten in the Red Barn. The remembrance comforted him. At least he was still in touch with the tangible and sane world.

But the strain was obviously getting him down. It was time to put his mind to his problem. He had always had a good mind, too good for his job. That, of course, was why the other staff resented him. Now was the time to use it. What, exactly, was he worrying about? A woman had been murdered. Whose fault had it been? Weren't there a number of people who shared the responsibility?

That blonde tart, for one, who had lent them the flat. The husband, who had been so easily fooled. The boy, who had enticed her away from her duty to husband and children. The victim herself – particularly the victim. The wages of sin are death. Well, she had taken her wages now. One man hadn't been enough for her.

Gabriel pictured again that dim shadow against the bedroom curtains, the raised arms as she drew Speller's head down to her breast. Filthy. Disgusting. Dirty. The adjectives smeared his mind. Well, she and her lover had taken their fun. It was right that both of them should pay for it. He, Ernest Gabriel, wasn't concerned. It had only been by the merest chance that he had seen them from that upper window, only by chance that he had seen Speller knock and go away again.

Justice was being served. He had sensed its majesty, the beauty of its essential rightness, at Speller's trial. And he, Gabriel, was a part of it. If he spoke now, an adulterer might even go free. His duty was clear. The temptation to speak had gone for ever.

It was in this mood that he stood with the small silent crowd outside the prison on the morning of Speller's execution. At the first stroke of eight, he, like the other men present, took off his hat. Staring up at the sky high above the prison walls, he felt again the warm exultation of his authority and power. It was on his behalf, it was at his, Gabriel's, bidding that the nameless hangman inside was exercising his dreadful craft . . .

But that was sixteen years ago. Four months after the trial the firm, expanding and conscious of the need for a better address, had moved from Camden Town to the north of London. Gabriel had moved with it. He was one of the few people on the staff who remembered the old building. Clerks came and went so quickly nowadays; there was no sense of loyalty to the job.

When Gabriel retired at the end of the year, only Mr Bootman and the porter would remain from the old Camden Town days. Sixteen years. Sixteen years of the same job, the same bedsitting room, the same half-tolerant dislike on the part of the staff. But he had had his moment of power. He recalled it now, looking round the small sordid sitting room with its peeling wallpaper, its stained boards. It had looked different sixteen years ago.

He remembered where the sofa had stood, the very spot where she had died. He remembered other things – the pounding of his heart as he made his way across the asphalt; the quick knock; the sidling through the half-opened door before she could realise it wasn't her lover; the naked body cowering back into the sitting room; the taut white throat; the thrust with his filing bodkin that was as smooth as puncturing soft rubber. The steel had gone in so easily, so sweetly.

And there was something else which he had done to her. But that was something it was better not to remember. And afterwards he had taken the bodkin back to the office, holding it under the tap in the bathroom until no spot of blood could have remained. Then he had replaced it in his desk drawer with half a dozen identical others. There had been nothing to distinguish it anymore, even to his eyes.

It had all been so easy. The only blood had been a gush on his right cuff as he withdrew the bodkin. And he had burned the coat in the office furnace. He still recalled the blast on his face as he thrust it in, and the spilled cinders like sand under his feet.

There had been nothing left to him but the key of the flat. He had seen it on the sitting-room table and had taken it away with him. He drew it now from his pocket and compared it with the key from the estate agent, laying them side by side on his outstretched palm. Yes, they were identical. They had had another one cut, but no one had bothered to change the lock.

He stared at the key, trying to recall the excitement of those weeks when he had been both judge and executioner. But he could feel nothing. It was all so long ago. He had been fifty then; now he was sixty-six. It was too old for feeling. And then he recalled the words of Mr Bootman. It was, after all, a very commonplace murder.

On Monday morning the girl in the estate office, clearing the mail from the letter box, called to the manager.

'That's funny! The old chap who took the key to the Camden Town flat has returned the wrong one. This hasn't got our label on it. Unless he pulled it off. Cheek! But why would he do that?'

She took the key over to the manager's desk, dumping his pile of letters in front of him. He glanced at it casually.

'That's the right key, anyway – it's the only one of that type we still have. Probably the label worked loose and fell off. You should put them on more carefully.'

'But I did!' Outraged, the girl wailed her protest. The manager winced.

'Then label it again, put it back on the board, and for God's sake don't fuss, that's a good girl.'

She glanced at him again, ready to argue. Then she shrugged. Come to think of it, he had always been a bit odd about that Camden Town flat.

'OK, Mr Morrisey,' she said.

The Boxdale Inheritance

'You see, my dear Adam,' explained the Canon gently, as he walked with Chief Superintendent Dalgliesh under the vicarage elms, 'useful as the legacy would be to us, I wouldn't feel happy in accepting it if Great Aunt Allie came by her money in the first place by wrongful means.'

What the Canon meant was that he and his wife wouldn't be happy to inherit Great Aunt Allie's fifty thousand pounds if, sixty-seven years earlier, she had poisoned her elderly husband with arsenic in order to get it. As Great Aunt Allie had been accused and acquitted of just that charge in a 1902 trial which, for her Hampshire neighbours, had rivalled the Coronation as a public spectacle, the Canon's scruples were not altogether irrelevant. Admittedly, thought Dalgliesh, most people faced with the prospect of fifty thousand pounds would be happy to subscribe to the commonly held convention that, once an English Court has pronounced its verdict, the final truth of the matter had been established once and for all. There may possibly be a higher judicature in the next world but hardly in this. And so Hubert Boxdale would normally be happy

P. D. JAMES

to believe. But, faced with the prospect of an unexpected fortune, his scrupulous conscience was troubled. The gentle but obstinate voice went on:

'Apart from the moral principle of accepting tainted money, it wouldn't bring us happiness. I often think of that poor woman, driven restlessly round Europe in her search for peace, of that lonely life and unhappy death.'

Dalgliesh recalled that Great Aunt Allie had moved in a predictable pattern with her retinue of servants, current lover and general hangers-on from one luxury Riviera hotel to the next, with stays in Paris or Rome as the mood suited her. He was not sure that this orderly programme of comfort and entertainment could be described as being restlessly driven round Europe or that the old lady had been primarily in search of peace. She had died, he recalled, by falling overboard from a millionaire's yacht during a rather wild party given by him to celebrate her eighty-eighth birthday. It was perhaps not an edifying death by the Canon's standards but Dalgliesh doubted whether she had, in fact, been unhappy at the time. Great Aunt Allie (it was impossible to think of her by any other name), if she had been capable of coherent thought, would probably have pronounced it a very good way to go.

But this was hardly a point of view he could put forward comfortably to his present companion.

Canon Hubert Boxdale was Chief Superintendent

Adam Dalgliesh's godfather. Dalgliesh's father had been his Oxford contemporary and lifelong friend. He had been an admirable godfather: affectionate, uncensorious, genuinely concerned. In Dalgliesh's childhood, he had always been mindful of birthdays and imaginative about a small boy's preoccupations and desires.

Dalgliesh was very fond of him and privately thought him one of the few really good men he had known. It was only surprising that the Canon had managed to live to seventy-one in a carnivorous world in which gentleness, humility and unworldliness are hardly conducive to survival, let alone success. But his goodness had in some sense protected him. Faced with such manifest innocence, even those who exploited him, and they were not a few, extended some of the protection and compassion they might show to the slightly subnormal.

'Poor old darling,' his daily woman would say, pocketing pay for six hours when she had worked five and helping herself to a couple of eggs from his refrigerator. 'He's really not fit to be let out alone.' It had surprised the then young and slightly priggish Detective Constable Dalgliesh to realise that the Canon knew perfectly well about the hours and the eggs, but thought that Mrs Copthorne, with five children and an indolent husband, needed both more than he did. He also knew that if he started paying for five hours she would promptly work only four and extract another two eggs, and that this small and only dishonesty was somehow necessary to her self-esteem. He was good. But he was not a fool.

He and his wife were, of course, poor. But they were not unhappy; indeed it was a word impossible to associate with the Canon. The death of his two sons in the 1939 war had saddened but not destroyed him. But he had anxieties. His wife was suffering from disseminated sclerosis and was finding it increasingly hard to manage. There were comforts and appliances which she would need. He was now, belatedly, about to retire and his pension would be small. A legacy of fifty thousand pounds would enable them both to live in comfort for the rest of their lives and would also, Dalgliesh had no doubt, give them the pleasure of doing more for their various lame dogs. Really, he thought, the Canon was an almost embarrassingly deserving candidate for a modest fortune. Why couldn't the dear, silly old noodle take the cash and stop worrying? He said cunningly: 'Great Aunt Allie was found Not Guilty, you know, by an English jury. And it all happened nearly seventy years ago. Couldn't you bring yourself to accept their verdict?'

But the Canon's scrupulous mind was totally impervious to such sly innuendoes. Dalgliesh told himself that he should have remembered what, as a small boy, he had discovered about Uncle Hubert's conscience – that it operated as a warning bell and that, unlike most people, Uncle Hubert never pretended that it hadn't sounded or that he hadn't heard it or that, having heard it, something must be wrong with the mechanism.

'Oh, I did, while she was alive. We never met after my grandfather's death, you know. I didn't wish to force myself on her. After all, she was a wealthy woman. My grandfather made a new will on his marriage and left her all he possessed. Our ways of life were very different. But I usually wrote briefly at Christmas and she sent a card in reply. I wanted to keep some contact in case, one day, she might want someone to turn to, and would remember that I am a priest.'

And why should she want that, thought Dalgliesh. To clear her conscience? Was that what the dear old boy had in mind? So he must have had some doubts from the beginning. But of course he had; Dalgliesh knew something of the story, and the general feeling of the family and friends was that Great Aunt Allie had been extremely lucky to escape the gallows.

His own father's view, expressed with reticence, reluctance and compassion, had not in essentials differed from that given by a local reporter at the time: 'How on earth did she expect to get away with it? Damned lucky to escape topping if you ask me.'

'The news of the legacy came as a complete surprise?' Dalgliesh asked the Canon.

'Indeed, yes. I saw her just once at that first and only Christmas, six weeks after her marriage, when my grandfather died. We always talk of her as Great Aunt Allie but in fact, as you know, she married my grandfather. But it seemed impossible to think of her as a step-grandmother.

'There was the usual family gathering at Colebrook Croft at the time I was there with my parents and my twin sisters. I was barely four and the twins were just eight months old. I can remember nothing of my grandfather or of his wife. After the murder – if one has to use that dreadful word – my mother returned home with us children, leaving my father to cope with the police, the solicitors and the newsmen. It was a terrible time for him. I don't think I was even told that my grandfather was dead until about a year later. My old nurse, Nellie, who had been given Christmas as a holiday to visit her own family, told me that, soon after my return home. I asked her if Grandfather was now young and beautiful for always. She, poor woman, took it as a sign of infant prognostication and piety. Poor Nellie was sadly superstitious and sentimental, I'm afraid. But I knew nothing of Grandfather's death at the time and certainly can recall nothing of that Christmas visit or of my new step-grandmother. Mercifully, I was little more than a baby when the murder was done.'

'She was a music-hall artist, wasn't she?' asked Dalgliesh.

'Yes, and a very talented one. My grandfather met

her when she was working with a partner in a hall in Cannes. He had gone to the South of France, with his man-servant, for his health. I understood that she extracted a gold watch from his chain and, when he claimed it, told him that he was English, had recently suffered from a stomach ailment, had two sons and a daughter, and was about to have a wonderful surprise. It was all correct except that his only daughter had died in childbirth leaving him a granddaughter, Marguerite Goddard.'

'That was all easily guessable from Boxdale's voice and appearance,' said Dalgliesh. 'I can only suppose the surprise was the marriage?'

'It was certainly a surprise, and a most unpleasant one for the family. It is easy to deplore the snobbishness and the conventions of another age and, indeed, there was much in Edwardian England to deplore, but it was not a propitious marriage. I think of the difference in background, education and way of life, the lack of common interests. And there was the disparity of age. Grandfather had married a girl just three months younger than his own granddaughter. I cannot wonder that the family were concerned, that they felt that the union could not, in the end, contribute to the contentment or happiness of either party.'

And that was putting it charitably, thought Dalgliesh. The marriage certainly hadn't contributed to their happiness. From the point of view of the family, it had been a disaster. He recalled hearing of an incident when the local vicar and his wife, a couple who had actually dined at Colebrook Croft on the night of the murder, first called on the bride. Apparently old Augustus Boxdale had introduced her, saying: 'Meet the prettiest little variety artiste in the business. Took a gold watch and notecase off me without any trouble. Would have had the elastic out of my pants if I hadn't watched out. Anyway, she stole my heart, didn't you, sweetheart?'

All this was accompanied by a hearty slap on the rump and a squeal of delight from the lady who had promptly demonstrated her skill by extracting the Reverend Arthur Venables' bunch of keys from his left ear.

Dalgliesh thought it tactful not to remind the Canon of this story.

'What do you wish me to do, Sir?' he enquired.

'It's asking a great deal, I know, when you're so busy. But if I had your assurance that you believed in Aunt Allie's innocence, I should feel happy about accepting the bequest. I wondered if it would be possible for you to see the records of the trial. Perhaps it would give you a clue. You're so clever at this sort of thing.'

He spoke without flattery but with an innocent wonder at the strange vocations of men. Dalgliesh was, indeed, very clever at this sort of thing. A dozen or so men at present occupying security wings in HM prisons could testify to Chief Superintendent Dalgliesh's cleverness as, indeed, could a handful of others walking free whose defending counsel had been in their own way as clever as Chief Superintendent Dalgliesh. But to re-examine a case over sixty years old seemed to require clairvoyance rather than cleverness. The trial judge and both learned counsels had been dead for over fifty years. Two world wars had taken their toll. Four reigns had passed. It was highly probable that, of those who had slept under the roof of Colebrook Croft on that fateful Boxing Day night of 1901, only the Canon still survived. But the old man was troubled and had sought his help, and Dalgliesh, with a day or two's leave due to him, had the time to give it.

'I'll do what I can,' he promised.

The transcript of a trial which had taken place sixty-seven years ago took time and trouble to obtain even for a Chief Superintendent of the Metropolitan Police. It provided little comfort for the Canon. Mr Justice Bellows had summed up with that avuncular simplicity with which he was wont to address juries, regarding them as a panel of well-intentioned but cretinous children. And the facts could have been comprehended by any child. Part of the summing-up set them out with lucidity:

'And so, gentlemen of the jury, we come to the night

– 85 –

of December 26th. Mr Augustus Boxdale, who had perhaps indulged a little unwisely on Christmas Day, had
retired to bed in his dressing room after luncheon, suffering from a recurrence of the slight indigestive trouble
which had afflicted him for most of his life. You will
have heard that he had taken luncheon with the members of his family and ate nothing which they, too, did
not eat. You may feel you can acquit luncheon of anything worse than over-richness.

'Dinner was served at 8 p.m. promptly, as was the custom at Colebrook Croft. There were present at that meal
Mrs Augustus Boxdale, the deceased's bride; his elder
son, Captain Maurice Boxdale, with his wife; his younger son, the Reverend Henry Boxdale, with his wife; his
granddaughter Miss Marguerite Goddard; and two
neighbours, the Reverend and Mrs Arthur Venables.

'You have heard how the accused took only the first
course at dinner, which was ragout of beef, and then, at
about 8.20, left the dining room to sit with her husband.
Shortly after nine o'clock she rang for the parlour maid,
Mary Huddy, and ordered a basin of gruel to be brought
up to Mr Boxdale. You have heard that the deceased was
fond of gruel, and indeed as prepared by Mrs Muncie,
the cook, it sounds a most nourishing dish for an elderly
gentleman of weak digestion.

'You have heard Mrs Muncie describe how she prepared the gruel according to Mrs Beaton's admirable

recipe and in the presence of Mary Huddy in case, as she said, "The master should take a fancy to it when I'm not at hand and you have to make it." After the gruel had been prepared, Mrs Muncie tasted it with a spoon and Mary Huddy carried it upstairs to the main bed-room together with a jug of water to thin the gruel if it were too strong. As she reached the door, Mrs Boxdale came out, her hands full of stockings and underclothes. She has told you that she was on her way to the bath-room to wash them through. She asked the girl to put the basin of gruel on the washstand by the window and Mary Huddy did so in her presence. Miss Huddy has told us that at the time she noticed the bowl of flypapers soaking in water and she knew that this solution was one used by Mrs Boxdale as a cosmetic wash. Indeed, all the women who spent that evening in the house, with the exception of Mrs Venables, have told you that they knew that it was Mrs Boxdale's practice to prepare this solution of flypapers.

'Mary Huddy and the accused left the bedroom together and you have heard the evidence of Mrs Muncie that Miss Huddy returned to the kitchen after an absence of only a few minutes. Shortly after nine o'clock, the ladies left the dining room and entered the drawing room to take coffee. At 9.15 p.m., Miss God-dard excused herself to the company and said that she would go to see if her grandfather needed anything.

The time is established precisely because the clock struck the quarter-hour as she left and Mrs Venables commented on the sweetness of its chime. You have also heard Mrs Venables' evidence and the evidence of Mrs Maurice Boxdale and Mrs Henry Boxdale that none of the ladies left the drawing room during the evening, and Mr Venables has testified that the three gentlemen remained together until Miss Goddard appeared about three-quarters of an hour after to inform them that her grandfather had become very ill and to request that the doctor be sent for immediately.

'Miss Goddard has told you that, when she entered her grandfather's room, he was just finishing his gruel and was grumbling about its taste. She got the impression that this was merely a protest at being deprived of his dinner rather than that he genuinely considered there was something wrong with the gruel. At any rate, he finished most of it and appeared to enjoy it despite his grumbles.

'You have heard Miss Goddard describe how, after her grandfather had had as much as he wanted of the gruel, she took the bowl next door and left it on the washstand. She then returned to her grandfather's bedroom and Mr Boxdale, his wife and his granddaughter played three-handed whist for about three-quarters of an hour.

'At ten o'clock Mr Augustus Boxdale complained of feeling very ill. He suffered from griping pains in the stomach, from sickness and from looseness of the bowels. As soon as the symptoms began Miss Goddard went downstairs to let her uncles know that her grandfather was worse and to ask that Doctor Eversley should be sent for urgently. Doctor Eversley has given you his evidence. He arrived at Colebrook Croft at 10.30 p.m. when he found his patient very distressed and weak. He treated the symptoms and gave what relief he could but Mr Augustus Boxdale died shortly before midnight.

'Gentlemen of the jury, you have heard Marguerite Goddard describe how, as her grandfather's paroxysms increased in intensity, she remembered the gruel and wondered whether it could have disagreed with him in some way. She mentioned this possibility to her elder uncle, Captain Maurice Boxdale. Captain Boxdale has told you how he handed the bowl with its residue of gruel to Doctor Eversley with the request that the doctor should lock it in a cupboard in the library, seal the lock and keep the key. You have heard how the contents of the bowl were later analysed and with what results.'

An extraordinary precaution for the gallant captain to have taken, thought Dalgliesh, and a most perspicacious young woman. Was it by chance or by design that the bowl hadn't been taken down to be washed up as soon as the old man had finished with it? Why was it, he wondered, that Marguerite Goddard hadn't rung for the parlour maid and requested her to remove it? Miss

Goddard appeared the only other suspect. He wished he knew more about her.

But, except for those main protagonists, the characters in the drama did not emerge very clearly from the trial report. Why, indeed, should they? The British accusatorial system of trial is designed to answer one question: is the accused guilty beyond reasonable doubt of the crime charged? Exploration of the nuances of personality, speculation and gossip have no place in the witness box. The two Boxdale brothers came out as very dull fellows indeed. They and their estimable, respectable, sloping-bosomed wives had sat at dinner in full view of each other from eight until after nine o'clock (a substantial meal, that dinner) and had said so in the witness box, more or less in identical words. The ladies' bosoms might have been heaving with far from estimable emotions of dislike, envy, embarrassment or resentment of the interloper. If so, they didn't tell the court.

But the two brothers and their wives were clearly innocent, even if a detective of that time could have conceived of the guilt of gentlefolk so well respected, so eminently respectable. Even their impeccable alibis had a nice touch of social and sexual distinction. The Reverend Arthur Venables had vouched for the gentlemen, his good wife for the ladies. Besides, what motive had they? They could no longer gain financially by the old man's death. If anything, it was in their interests to keep him alive in the hope that disillusion with his marriage or a return to sanity might occur to cause him to change his will. So far Dalgliesh had learned nothing that could cause him to give the Canon the assurance for which he hoped.

It was then that he remembered Aubrey Glatt. Glatt was a wealthy amateur criminologist who had made a study of all the notable Victorian and Edwardian poison cases. He was not interested in anything earlier or later, being as obsessively wedded to his period as any serious historian, which indeed he had some claim to call himself. He lived in a Georgian house in Winchester – his affection for the Victorian and Edwardian age did not extend to its architecture – and was only three miles from Colebrook Croft. A visit to the London Library disclosed that he hadn't written a book on the case but it was improbable that he had totally neglected a crime close at hand and so in period. Dalgliesh had occasionally helped him with the technical details of police procedure. Glatt, in response to a telephone call, was happy to return the favour with the offer of afternoon tea and information.

Tea was served in his elegant drawing room by a parlour maid wearing a frilly cap with streamers. Dalgliesh wondered what wage Glatt paid her to persuade her to wear it. She looked as if she could have played a role in any of his favourite Victorian dreams and Dalgliesh had an uncomfortable thought that arsenic might be dispensed with the cucumber sandwiches. Glatt nibbled away and was expansive.

'It's interesting that you should have taken this sudden and, if I may say so, somewhat inexplicable interest in the Boxdale murder; I got out my notebook on the case only yesterday. Colebrook Croft is being demolished to make way for a new housing estate and I thought I would visit it for the last time. The family, of course, haven't lived there since the 1914–18 war. Architecturally, it's completely undistinguished but one grieves to see it go. We might drive over after tea if you are agreeable.

'I never wrote my book on the case, you know. I planned a work entitled *The Colebrook Croft Mystery, or Who Killed Augustus Boxdale?* But the answer was all too obvious.'

'No real mystery?' suggested Dalgliesh.

'Who else could it have been but Allegra Boxdale? She was born Allegra Porter, you know. Do you think her mother could have been thinking of Byron? I imagine not. There's a picture of her on page two of the notebook by the way, taken by a photographer in Cannes on her wedding day. I call it beauty and the beast.'

The old photograph had scarcely faded and Great Aunt Allie half-smiled at Dalgliesh across nearly seventy years. Her broad face with its wide mouth and rather snub nose was framed by two wings of dark hair swept high and topped, in the fashion of the day, by an enormous flowered hat. The features were too coarse for real beauty but the eyes were magnificent, deep set and well spaced, and the chin round and determined. Beside this vital young Amazon poor Augustus Boxdale, clutching his bride as if for support, was but a very frail and undersized beast. Their pose was unfortunate. She almost looked as if she were about to fling him over her shoulder.

Glatt shrugged. 'The face of a murderess? I've known less likely ones. Her counsel suggested, of course, that the old man had poisoned his own gruel during the short time she left it on the washstand to cool while she visited the bathroom. But why should he? All the evidence suggests that he was in a state of post-nuptial euphoria, poor senile old booby. Our Augustus was in no hurry to leave this world, particularly by such an agonising means. Besides, I doubt whether he even knew the gruel was there. He was in bed next door in his dressing room, remember.'

Dalgliesh asked: 'What about Marguerite Goddard? There's no evidence about the exact time when she entered the bedroom.'

'I thought you'd get onto that. She could have arrived while her step-grandmother was in the bathroom, poisoned the gruel, hidden herself either in the main bedroom or elsewhere until it had been taken in to Augustus, then joined her grandfather and his bride as if she had just come upstairs. It's possible, I admit. But it is unlikely. She was less inconvenienced than any of the family by her grandfather's second marriage. Her mother was Augustus Boxdale's eldest child who married, very young, a wealthy patent medicine manufacturer. She died in childbirth and the husband only survived her by a year. Marguerite Goddard was an heiress. She was also most advantageously engaged to Captain the Honourable John Brize-Lacey. Marguerite Goddard, young, beautiful, in possession of the Goddard fortune, not to mention the Goddard emeralds and the eldest son of a lord, was hardly a serious suspect. In my view defence counsel, that was Roland Gort Lloyd, remember, was wise to leave her strictly alone.'

'A memorable defence, I believe.'

'Magnificent. There's no doubt Allegra Boxdale owed her life to Gort Lloyd. I know that concluding speech by heart:

' "Gentlemen of the jury, I beseech you in the sacred name of Justice to consider what you are asked to do. It is your responsibility, and yours alone, to decide the fate of this young woman. She stands before you now, young, vibrant, glowing with health, the years stretching before her with their promise and their hopes. It is in your power to cut off all this as you might top a nettle with one swish of your cane. To condemn her to the slow torture of those last waiting weeks; to that last dreadful walk; to heap calumny on her name; to dese-crate those few happy weeks of marriage with the man who loved her so greatly; and to cast her into the final darkness of an ignominious grave."

'Pause for dramatic effect. Then the crescendo in that magnificent voice. "And on what evidence, gentlemen? I ask you." Another pause. Then the thunder. "On what evidence?"'

'A powerful defence,' said Dalgliesh. 'But I wonder how it would go down with a modern judge and jury.'

'Well, it went down very effectively with that 1902 jury. Of course, the abolition of capital punishment has rather cramped the more histrionic style. I'm not sure that the reference to topping nettles was in the best of taste. But the jury got the message. They decided that, on the whole, they preferred not to have the responsibil-ity of sending the accused to the gallows. They were out six hours reaching their verdict and it was greeted with some applause. If any of those worthy citizens had been asked to wager five pounds of their own good money on her innocence, I suspect that it would have been a differ-ent matter. Allegra Boxdale had helped him, of course. The Criminal Evidence Act, passed three years earlier, enabled him to put her in the witness box. She wasn't an actress of a kind for nothing. Somehow, she managed to persuade the jury that she had genuinely loved the old man.'

'Perhaps she had,' suggested Dalgliesh. 'I don't suppose there had been much kindness in her life. And he was kind.'

'No doubt, no doubt. But love!' Glatt was impatient. 'My dear Dalgliesh! He was a singularly ugly old man of sixty-nine. She was an attractive girl of twenty-one!'

Dalgliesh doubted whether love, that iconoclastic passion, was susceptible to this kind of simple arithmetic but he didn't argue. Glatt went on: 'The prosecution couldn't suggest any other romantic attachment. The police got in touch with her previous partner, of course. He was discovered to be a bald, undersized little man, sharp as a weasel, with a buxom wife and five children. He had moved down the coast after the partnership broke up and was now working with a new girl. He said regretfully that she was coming along nicely, thank you gentlemen, but would never be a patch on Allie and that, if Allie got her neck out of the noose and ever wanted a job, she knew where to come. It was obvious, even to the most suspicious policeman, that his interest was professional. As he said: "What was a grain or two of arsenic between friends?"

'The Boxdales had no luck after the trial. Captain Maurice Boxdale was killed in 1916 leaving no children, and the Reverend Edward lost his wife and their twin daughters in the 1918 influenza epidemic. He survived until 1932. The boy, Hubert, may still be alive, but I doubt it. That family always were a sickly lot.

'My greatest achievement, incidentally, was in tracing Marguerite Goddard. I hadn't realised that she was still alive. She never married Brize-Lacey or, indeed, anyone else. He distinguished himself in the 1914–18 war, came successfully through, and eventually married an eminently suitable young woman, the sister of a brother officer. He inherited the title in 1925 and died in 1953. But Marguerite Goddard may be alive now for all I know. She may even be living in the same modest Bournemouth hotel where I found her. Not that my efforts in tracing her were rewarded. She absolutely refused to see me. That's the note that she sent out to me, by the way. Just there.'

It was meticulously pasted into the notebook in its chronological order and carefully annotated. Aubrey Glatt was a natural researcher; Dalgliesh couldn't help wondering whether this passion for accuracy might not have been more rewarding spent other than in the careful documentation of murder.

The note was written in an elegant upright hand, the strokes black and very thin but clear and unwavering.

Miss Goddard presents her compliments to Mr Aubrey Glatt. She did not murder her grandfather and has neither the time nor the inclination to gratify his curiosity by discussing the person who did.

Aubrey Glatt said: 'After that extremely disobliging note, I felt there was really no point in going on with the book.'

Glatt's passion for Edwardian England evidently extended to a wider field than its murders, and they drove to Colebrook Croft high above the green Hampshire lanes in an elegant 1910 Daimler. Aubrey wore a thin tweed coat and deer-stalker hat and looked, Dalgliesh thought, rather like Sherlock Holmes, with himself as attendant Watson.

'We are only just in time, my dear Dalgliesh,' he said when they arrived. 'The engines of destruction are assembled. That ball on a chain looks like the eyeball of God, ready to strike. Let us make our number with the attendant artisans. You will have no wish to trespass, will you?'

The work of demolition had not yet begun but the inside of the house had been stripped and plundered, the great rooms echoed to their footsteps like gaunt and deserted barracks after the final retreat. They moved from room to room, Glatt mourning the forgotten glories of an age he had been born too late to enjoy; Dalgliesh with his mind on the somewhat more immediate and practical concerns.

The design of the house was simple and formalised. The first floor, on which were most of the main bedrooms, had a long corridor running the whole length of the facade. The master bedroom was at the southern end with two large windows giving a distant view of Winchester Cathedral tower. A communicating door led to a small dressing room.

The main corridor had a row of four identical large windows. The brass curtain rods and wooden rings had been removed (they were collector's items now) but the ornate carved pelmets were still in place. Here must have hung pairs of heavy curtains giving cover to anyone who wished to slip out of view. And Dalgliesh noted with interest that one of the windows was exactly opposite the door of the main bedroom. By the time they had left Colebrook Croft and Glatt had dropped him at Winchester Station, Dalgliesh was beginning to formulate a theory.

His next move was to trace Marguerite Goddard if she were still alive. It took him nearly a week of weary searching, a frustrating trail along the South Coast from hotel to hotel. Almost everywhere his enquiries were met with defensive hostility. It was the usual story of a very old lady who had become more demanding, arrogant and eccentric as her health and fortune waned; an unwelcome embarrassment to manager and fellow guests alike. The hotels were all modest, a few almost sordid. What, he wondered, had become of the legendary Goddard fortune?

From the last landlady he learned that Miss Goddard

had become ill, really very sick indeed, and had been removed six months previously to the local district general hospital. And it was there that he found her.

The ward sister was surprisingly young, a petite, dark-haired girl with a tired face and challenging eyes.

'Miss Goddard is very ill. We've put her in one of the side wards. Are you a relative? If so, you're the first one who has bothered to call and you're lucky to be in time. When she is delirious she seems to expect a Captain Brize-Lacey to call. You're not he, are you?'

'Captain Brize-Lacey will not be calling. No, I'm not a relative. She doesn't even know me. But I would like to visit her if she's well enough and is willing to see me. Could you please give her this note.'

He couldn't force himself on a defenceless and dying woman. She still had the right to say no. He was afraid she would refuse him. And if she did, he might never learn the truth. He wrote four words on the back page of his diary, signed them, tore out the page, folded it and handed it to the sister.

She was back very shortly.

'She'll see you. She's weak, of course, and very old but she's perfectly lucid now. Only please don't tire her.'

'I'll try not to stay too long.'

The girl laughed:

'Don't worry. She'll throw you out soon enough if she gets bored. The chaplain and the Red Cross librarian have a terrible time with her. Third floor on the left. There's a stool to sit on under the bed. We will ring the bell at the end of visiting time.'

She bustled off, leaving him to find his own way. The corridor was very quiet. At the far end, he could glimpse through the open door of the main ward the regimented rows of beds, each with its pale blue coverlet, the bright glow of flowers on some of the tables, and the laden visitors making their way in pairs to each bedside. There was a faint buzz of welcome, a hum of conversation. But no one was visiting the side wards. Here, in the silence of the sterile corridor, Dalgliesh could smell death.

The woman, propped high against the pillows in the third room on the left, no longer looked human. She lay rigidly, her long arms disposed like sticks on the coverlet. This was a skeleton clothed with a thin membrane of flesh beneath whose yellow transparency the tendons and veins were as plainly visible as an anatomist's model. She was nearly bald and the high-domed skull under its spare down of hair was as brittle and vulnerable as a child's. Only the eyes still held life, burning in their deep sockets with an animal vitality. But when she spoke her voice was distinctive and unwavering, evoking as her appearance never could the memory of imperious youth.

She took up his note and read aloud four words:

'"It was the child." You are right, of course. The four-year-old Hubert Boxdale killed his grandfather. You signed this note Adam Dalgliesh. There was no Dalgliesh connected with the case.'

'I am a detective of the Metropolitan Police. But I'm not here in any official capacity. I have known about this case for a number of years from a dear friend. I have a natural curiosity to learn the truth. And I have formed a theory.'

'And now, like that poseur Aubrey Glatt, you want to write a book?'

'No. I shall tell no one. You have my promise.'

Her voice was ironic.

'Thank you. I am a dying woman, Mr Dalgliesh. I tell you that, not to invite your sympathy which it would be an impertinence for you to offer and which I neither want nor require, but to explain why it no longer matters to me what you say or do. But I, too, have a natural curiosity. Your note, cleverly, was intended to provoke it. I should like to know how you discovered the truth.'

Dalgliesh drew the visitor's stool from under the bed and sat down beside her. She did not look at him. The skeleton hands still holding his note did not move.

'Everyone in Colebrook Croft who could have killed Augustus Boxdale was accounted for, except the one person whom nobody considered, the small boy. He was an intelligent, articulate child. He was almost certainly left to his own devices. His nurse did not accompany the family to Colebrook Croft and the servants who were there over Christmas had extra work and also the care of the delicate twin girls. The boy probably spent much time with his grandfather and the new bride. She, too, was lonely and disregarded. He could have trotted around with her as she went about her various activities. He could have watched her making her arsenical face wash and, when he asked, as a child will, what it was for, could have been told "to make me young and beautiful". He loved his grandfather but he must have known that the old man was neither young nor beautiful. Suppose he woke up on that Boxing Day night overfed and excited after the Christmas festivities? Suppose he went to Allegra Boxdale's room in search of comfort and companionship and saw there the basin of gruel and the arsenical mixture together on the washstand? Suppose he decided that here was something he could do for his grandfather?'

The voice from the bed said quietly:

'And suppose someone stood unnoticed in the doorway and watched him.'

'So you were behind the window curtains on the landing looking through the open door?'

'Of course. He knelt on the chair, two chubby hands clasping the bowl of poison, pouring it with infinite care into his grandfather's gruel. I watched while he

replaced the linen cloth over the basin, got down from
the chair, replaced it with careful art against the wall
and trotted out into the corridor and back to the nurs-
ery. About three seconds later, Allegra came out of the
bathroom and I watched while she carried the gruel in
to my grandfather. A second later I went into the main
bedroom. The bowl of poison had been a little heavy for
Hubert's small hands to manage and I saw that a small
pool had been spilt on the polished top of the washstand.
I mopped it up with my handkerchief. Then I poured
some of the water from the jug into the poison bowl to
bring up the level. It only took a couple of seconds and
I was ready to join Allegra and my grandfather in the
bedroom and sit with him while he ate his gruel.

'I watched him die without pity and without remorse.
I think I hated them both equally. The grandfather
who had adored, petted and indulged me all through
my childhood and deteriorated into this disgusting old
lecher, unable to keep his hands off this woman even
when I was in the room. He had rejected me and his
family, jeopardised my engagement, made our name a
laughing stock in the county, and all for a woman that
my grandmother wouldn't have employed as a kitchen
maid. I wanted them both dead. And they were both
going to die. But it would be by other hands than mine.
I could deceive myself that it wasn't my doing.'

Dalgliesh asked: 'When did she find out?'

'She knew that evening. When my grandfather's agony began she went outside for the jug of water. She wanted a cool cloth for his head. It was then that she noticed that the level of water in the jug had fallen and that a small pool of liquid on the washstand had been mopped up. I should have realised that she would have seen that pool. She had been trained to register every detail. She thought at the time that Mary Huddy had spilt some of the water when she set down the tray and the gruel. But who but I could have mopped it up? And why?'

'And when did she face you with the truth?'

'Not until after the trial. Allegra had magnificent courage. She knew what was at stake. But she also knew what she stood to gain. She gambled with her life for a fortune.'

And then Dalgliesh understood what had happened to the Goddard inheritance.

'So she made you pay?'

'Of course. Every penny. The Goddard fortune, the Goddard emeralds. She lived in luxury for sixty-seven years on my money. She ate and dressed on my money. When she moved with her lovers from hotel to hotel it was on my money. She paid them with my money. And if she has left anything, which I doubt, it is my money. My grandfather left very little. He had been senile and had let money run through his fingers like sand.'

'And your engagement?'

'It was broken, you could say by mutual consent. A marriage, Mr Dalgliesh, is like any other legal contract. It is most successful when both parties are convinced they have a bargain. Captain Brize-Lacey was sufficiently discouraged by the scandal of a murder in the family. He was a proud and highly conventional man. But that alone might have been accepted with the Goddard fortune and the Goddard emeralds to deodorise the bad smell. But the marriage couldn't have succeeded if he had discovered that he had married socially beneath him, into a family with a major scandal and no compensating fortune.'

Dalgliesh said: 'Once you had begun to pay you had no choice but to go on. I see that. But why did you pay? She could hardly have told her story. It would have meant involving the child.'

'Oh no! That wasn't her plan at all. She never meant to involve the child. She was a sentimental woman and she was fond of Hubert. No, she intended to accuse me of murder outright. Then, if I decided to tell the truth, how would it help me? After all, I wiped up the spilled liquid, I topped up the bowl. She had nothing to lose remember, neither life nor reputation. They couldn't try her twice. That's why she waited until after the trial. It made her secure for ever.

'But what of me? In the circles in which I moved at

that time reputation was everything. She needed only to breathe the story in the ears of a few servants and I was finished. The truth can be remarkably tenacious. But it wasn't only reputation. I paid in the shadow of the gallows.'

Dalgliesh asked, 'But could she ever prove it?'

Suddenly she looked at him and gave an eerie screech of laughter. It tore at her throat until he thought the taut tendons would snap violently.

'Of course she could! You fool! Don't you understand? She took my handkerchief, the one I used to mop up the arsenic mixture. That was her profession, remember. Some time during that evening, perhaps when we were all crowding around the bed, two soft plump fingers insinuated themselves between the satin of my evening dress and my flesh and extracted that stained and damning piece of linen.'

She stretched out feebly towards the bedside locker. Dalgliesh saw what she wanted and pulled open the drawer. There on the top was a small square of very fine linen with a border of hand-stitched lace. He took it up. In the corner was her monogram delicately embroidered. And half of the handkerchief was still stiff and stained with brown.

She said: 'She left instructions with her solicitors that this was to be returned to me after her death. She always knew where I was. But now she's dead. And I shall soon follow. You may have the handkerchief, Mr Dalgliesh. It can be of no further use to either of us now.'

Dalgliesh put it in his pocket without speaking. As soon as possible he would see that it was burnt. But there was something else he had to say. 'Is there anything you would wish me to do? Is there anyone you want told, or to tell? Would you care to see a priest?'

Again there was that uncanny screech of laughter but softer now:

'There's nothing I can say to a priest. I only regret what I did because it wasn't successful. That is hardly the proper frame of mind for a good confession. But I bear her no ill will. One should be a good loser. But I've paid, Mr Dalgliesh. For sixty-seven years I've paid. And in this world, young man, the rich only pay once.'

She lay back as if suddenly exhausted. There was a silence for a moment. Then she said with sudden vigour:

'I believe your visit has done me good. I would be obliged if you'd return each afternoon for the next three days. I shan't trouble you after that.'

Dalgliesh extended his leave with some difficulty and stayed at a local inn. He saw her each afternoon. They never spoke again of the murder. And when he came punctually at 2.00 p.m. on the fourth day it was to be told that Miss Goddard had died peacefully in the night with apparently no trouble to anyone. She was, as she had said, a good loser.

A week later, Dalgliesh reported to the Canon.

'I was able to see a man who has made a detailed study of the case. I have read the transcript of the trial and visited Colebrook Croft. And I have seen one other person, closely connected with the case but who is now dead. I know you will want me to respect confidence and to say no more than I need.'

The Canon murmured his quiet assurance. Dalgliesh went on quickly:

'As a result I can give you my word that the verdict was a just verdict and that not one penny of your grandfather's fortune is coming to you through anyone's wrongdoing.'

He turned his face away and gazed out of the window. There was a long silence. The old man was probably giving thanks in his own way. Then Dalgliesh was aware of his godfather speaking. Something was being said about gratitude, about the time he had given up to the investigation.

'Please don't misunderstand me, Adam. But when the formalities have been completed I should like to donate something to a charity named by you, one close to your heart.'

Dalgliesh smiled. His contributions to charity were impersonal; a quarterly obligation discharged by banker's order. The Canon obviously regarded charities as so many old clothes; all were friends but some fitted better and were consequently more affectionately regarded than others.

But inspiration came:

'It's good of you to think of it, Sir. I rather liked what I learned about Great Aunt Allie. It would be pleasant to give something in her name. Isn't there a society for the assistance of retired and indigent variety artists, conjurers and so on?'

The Canon, predictably, knew that there was and could name it.

Dalgliesh said: 'Then I think, Canon, that Great Aunt Allie would have agreed that a donation in her name would be entirely appropriate.'

The Twelve Clues of Christmas

The figure who leaps from the side of the road in the darkness of a winter afternoon, frantically waving down the approaching motorist, is so much the creature of fiction that when it happened to the newly promoted Sergeant Adam Dalgliesh his first thought was that he had somehow become involved in one of those Christmas short stories written to provide a seasonal frisson for the readers of an upmarket weekly magazine. But the figure was real enough, the emergency apparently genuine.

Dalgliesh wound down the window of his MG Midget letting in a stream of cold December air, a swirl of soft snow and a male head.

'Thank God you've stopped! I've got to telephone the police. My uncle's committed suicide. I'm from Harkerville Hall.'

'Haven't you got a telephone?'

'If I had I wouldn't be stopping you. It's out of order. It often is. And now the car's packed up.'

Adam had noticed a telephone box on the outskirts of a village he had passed less than five minutes ago. On the other hand, he was only ten minutes' drive from his aunt's cottage on the Suffolk coast where he was to spend Christmas. But why intrude a not particularly agreeable stranger on her privacy? He said: 'I can drive you to a telephone box. I passed one just outside Wivenhaven.'

'Then hurry. It's urgent. He's dead.'

'Are you sure?'

'Of course I'm sure. He's cold and he isn't breathing and he's got no pulse.'

Dalgliesh was tempted to say, 'In that case there's no particular hurry,' but forbore.

The stranger's voice was harsh and didactic, and Adam suspected that his face might be equally unprepossessing. He was, however, wearing a heavy tweed coat with collar upturned and little was visible except a long nose. Adam leaned over to open the left-hand door and he got in. He was certainly genuine enough in the sense that he was obviously labouring under some emotion, but Adam detected more anxiety and chagrin than shock or grief.

His passenger said ungraciously: 'I'd better introduce myself. Helmut Harkerville, and I'm not German. My mother liked the name.'

There seemed no possible reply to this. Dalgliesh introduced himself and they drove in uncompanionable silence to the telephone box. Getting out, Harkerville said crossly: 'Oh God, I've forgotten the money.'

Dalgleish dug into his jacket pocket and handed over an assortment of coins, then followed him out to the telephone. The local police wouldn't relish being called out at 4.30 on Christmas Eve, and if this was some kind of hoax he preferred not to be an active participant. On the other hand, it was right to call his aunt to warn her that he might be delayed.

The first call took some minutes. Returning, Harkerville said with annoyance: 'They took it remarkably calmly. Anyone would think people in this county kill themselves routinely at Christmas.'

Dalgliesh said, 'East Anglians are robust. Family members are occasionally tempted, but most manage to resist.'

Adam's call completed, they came to the place where he had picked up his passenger. Harkerville said shortly: 'There's a right-hand turning here. It's less than a mile to Harkerville Hall.'

Driving in silence, it occurred to Adam that he might have a responsibility beyond dropping his passenger at the front door. He was, after all, a police officer. This wasn't his patch, but he ought to confirm that the corpse was indeed a corpse and beyond help, and to await the arrival of the local police. He put this proposition to his companion, quietly but firmly, and after a minute received a grudging acquiescence.

'Do what you like, but you're wasting your time. He's

left a note. This is Harkerville Hall, but if you're local you probably know it, at least by sight.'

Dalgliesh did know the hall by sight and its owner by reputation. It was a house difficult to avoid noticing. He reflected that today not even the most accommodating planning authority would have sanctioned its erection close to one of the most attractive stretches of the Suffolk coastline. In the 1870s a more indulgent system had prevailed. The then Harkerville had made his millions from dosing insomniacs, dyspeptics and the impotent with a mixture of opium, bicarbonate of soda and liquorice, and had retired to Suffolk to build his status symbol designed to impress the neighbours and inconvenience his staff. Its present owner was reputed to be equally rich, mean and reclusive.

Helmut said: 'I'm down for Christmas as usual with my sister Gertrude and my brother Carl. My wife isn't with us. Not feeling up to it. Oh, and there's a temporary cook, Mrs Dagworth. My uncle instructed me to advertise for her in the *Lady's Companion* and bring her down with us yesterday evening. His usual cook-housekeeper and Mavis the house parlour maid go home for Christmas.'

Having put Adam into the picture by this surely unnecessary recital of domestic arrangements, he relapsed into silence.

The hall came upon them with such suddenness that

Adam instinctively braked. It reared up in the head-lights, looking more like an aberration of the natural world than a human habitation. The architect, if archi-tect had indeed been employed, had begun his mon-strosity as a large, square, multi-windowed house in red brick and had then, under the impulse of a perverse creative frenzy, erected a huge ornamental porch more suitable for a cathedral, thrown out four large bay win-dows and adorned the roof with a turret at each corner and a central dome.

It had snowed all night, but the morning had been dry and very cold. Now, however, the first flakes were thickening, beginning to obliterate the double tyre marks in the car's headlights. Their approach was silent, and the house itself seemed deserted. Only the ground floor and an upper window showed a frail light shining through the slits of drawn curtains.

The great hall, oak-panelled and ill-lit, was cold. A cavernous fireplace contained only a two-bar electric fire, and a bunch of holly stuck behind a couple of heavy, undistinguished portraits enhanced rather than mitigat-ed the gloom. The man who let them in and who now pushed shut the solid oak door was clearly Carl Harker-ville. Like his sister, who came rushing forward, he had the Harkerville nose, bright suspicious eyes and a thin tight mouth. A second woman, standing at the edge of the group in stony disapproval, was not introduced, but was presumably the hired cook, although a thin plaster on her middle right finger suggested a certain incompetence with a knife. Her mean little mouth and dark suspicious eyes suggested that her mind was as tightly corseted as her body. Helmut's introduction of Adam as 'a sergeant of the Metropolitan Police' was received by his siblings with a wary silence, and by Mrs Dagworth with a quickly repressed gasp. When the family preceded Adam up to the bedroom she followed.

The room, also panelled in oak, was immense. The bed was an oak four-poster with a canopy, and the dead man lay on top of the counterpane. He was wearing only his pyjamas and there was a small sprig of dry holly, extremely prickly and with shrunken berries, stuck into the top buttonhole. The Harkerville nose stuck out, pitted and scarred like a ship's prow weathered by many voyages. The eyes were tight-closed as if by an effort of will. The gaping mouth was stuffed with what looked like Christmas pudding. His gnarled hands, the nails surprisingly long and gummed with ointment, were disposed across his stomach. On his head was a crown in red tissue paper, obviously from a cracker. The heavy bedside table held a lamp, switched on but giving a subdued light, an empty bottle of whisky, a labelled pill bottle, also empty, an open tin containing an obnoxious-smelling ointment labelled Harkerville's Hair Restorer, a small thermos-flask, a Christmas cracker which had been pulled, and a Christmas pudding still in its basin but with a lump gouged out of the top. There was also a note.

The message was handwritten in a surprisingly firm script. Dalgliesh read: 'I've been planning this for some time, and if you don't like it, you can put up with it. This, thank God, will be my last family Christmas. No more of Gertrude's stodgy Christmas pudding and overcooked turkey. No more ridiculous paper hats. No more holly indiscriminately stuck around the house. No more of your repellently ugly faces and mind-numbing company. I'm entitled to some peace and happiness. I'm going where I can get it, and my darling will be waiting for me.'

Helmut Harkerville said: 'He was always a practical joker, but you'd think he'd want to die with some dignity. Finding him like this was a terrible shock, particularly for my sister. But then Uncle never had any consideration for others.'

His brother said, with quiet reproof: 'Nil nisi bonum, Helmut, nil nisi bonum. He knows better now.'

Adam asked: 'Who found him?'

'I did,' said Helmut. 'Well, at least I was first up the ladder. We never have early morning tea here, but Uncle always took to bed a flask of strong coffee to drink in the morning with a tot of whisky. He's usually up early so when he didn't appear for breakfast by nine o'clock Mrs

Dagworth went to see if he was all right. She found the door locked, but he shouted out that he didn't want to be disturbed. My sister tried again when he didn't come down for lunch. When we couldn't make him hear we got out the ladder and climbed in through the window. The ladder's still in place.'

Mrs Dagworth was standing beside the bed in stiff disapproval. She said: 'I was employed to cook Christmas dinner for four. No one told me that the house was an unheated monstrosity and the owner suicidal. God knows how his usual cook manages. That kitchen hasn't been upgraded for eighty years. I tell you now, I'm not staying. As soon as the police arrive, I go. And I shall make a complaint to the *Lady's Companion*. You'll be lucky to get another cook.'

Helmut said: 'The last bus leaves for London early on Christmas Eve and there isn't another until Boxing Day. You'll have to stay until then, so you may as well do what you're paid to do, get on with some work.'

His brother said: 'And you can make a start by getting us some tea, hot and strong. I'm starved in here.'

Indeed the room was exceptionally cold. Gertrude said: 'It will be warm in the kitchen. Thank God for the Aga. We'll all go there.'

Dalgliesh had hoped for something a little more seasonal than tea and thought with longing of the excellent meal awaiting him at his aunt's cottage, the carefully chosen claret already open, the cracking and sea-tang of a driftwood fire. But the kitchen was at least warmer. The Aga was the only piece of reasonably modern equipment. The floor was stone-flagged, the double sink was stained and there was a huge dresser covering one wall loaded with an assortment of jugs, mugs, plates and tins, and several cupboards, the tops all similarly covered. On an overhead pulley a collection of tea towels, obviously washed but still stained, hung like depressing flags of truce.

Gertrude said: 'I brought down a Christmas cake. Perhaps we could cut that.'

Carl said quietly: 'I think not, Gertrude. I don't think I could stomach Christmas cake with Uncle lying dead. There are probably some biscuits in the usual tin.'

Mrs Dagworth, her face a mask of resentment, took a tin from the dresser labelled 'sugar' and began spooning out tea into the teapot, then burrowed in one of the cupboards and brought out a large red tin. The biscuits were old and soft. Dalgliesh declined them but was grateful for the tea when it came.

He said: 'When did you last see your uncle alive?'

It was Helmut who replied: 'He had supper with us last night. We didn't arrive till eight and naturally his cook had left nothing for us. She never does. But we'd brought some cold meat and salad and had that. Mrs Dagworth opened a tin of soup. At nine o'clock, immediately after the news, Uncle said he'd go to bed. No one saw or heard him again except Mrs Dagworth.'

Mrs Dagworth said: 'When I called him for breakfast and he shouted to me to go away, I heard him pull the cracker. So he was alive at nine or just after.'

Adam said: 'You're sure of the sound?'

'Of course I was. I know the sound of a cracker being pulled. It seemed a little odd so I went to the door and called out, "Are you all right Mr Harkerville?" He called back, "Of course I'm all right. Go away and stay away." That's the last time he spoke to anyone.'

Dalgliesh said: 'He must have been standing close to the door for you to hear him. It's solid wood.'

Mrs Dagworth flushed, then said angrily: 'Solid wood it may be, but I know what I heard. I heard the cracker and I heard him tell me to go away. Anyway, it's plain what's happened. You've got the suicide note, haven't you? It's in his handwriting.'

Adam said: 'I'll go upstairs and keep watch on the room. You'd better wait for the Suffolk police.'

There was no reason why he should keep watch on the room, and he half-expected them to protest. However, no one did and he climbed the stairs alone. He entered the bedroom and locked the door with the key which was still in the keyhole. Going over to the bed, he scrutinised the corpse carefully, smelt the ointment with a grimace of distaste and bent over the body. It was apparent that Harkerville had applied the grease liberally to his scalp before going to bed. The hands were lightly clenched but he could detect in the right palm a wodge of Christmas pudding. Rigor mortis was just beginning in the upper part of the body, but he gently raised the stiffening head and studied the pillow.

After examining the cracker he turned his attention to the note. Turning it over, he saw that the back of the paper was slightly brown as if it had been scorched. Going over to the immense grate, he saw that someone had been burning papers. There was a pyramid of white ash which still gave a faint heat to his exploring hand. The burning had been thorough except for one small segment of cardboard with what looked like a unicorn's horn, and a scrap of letter. The paper was thick and the few type-written words plain. He read: ', eight hundred pounds not unreasonable considering'. There was no more and he left both fragments in place.

To the right of the window, there was a heavy oak desk. It suggested that Cuthbert Harkerville had slept more peaceably with his important papers close to hand. The desk was unlocked but was completely empty except for some bundles of old receipted bills held together with rubber bands. The desktop and the mantelshelf were likewise empty. The huge wardrobe, smelling of mothballs, held only clothes.

Adam decided to take a look at the adjoining rooms,

not without qualms that this was trespass. The room occupied by Mrs Dagworth was as bleakly unfurnished as a prison cell, the only remarkable feature a mouldy stuffed bear holding a brass tray. Her unopened case lay on a bed too narrow for comfort and with a single hard pillow.

The room to the right was equally small, but the absent Mavis had at least imposed on it some trace of adolescent personality. Posters of film and pop stars were stuck on the walls. There was a battered but comfortable cane chair and the bed was covered with a quilted bedspread patterned with leaping lambs in pink and blue. The small rickety wardrobe was empty; Mavis had discarded her half-used make-up jars into the wastepaper basket and had slung on top of them a variety of old and soiled clothes.

Adam returned to the main bedroom and completed his unsuccessful search for two missing objects.

The village was four miles distant and it was half an hour before Constable Taplow arrived. He was a thick-set middle-aged man, his natural bulk enhanced by the layers of clothing he considered necessary for a cycle ride in December. Despite the fact that the snow had subsided, he insisted on wheeling his bicycle into the hall, to the obvious but silent disapproval of the family, leant it with care against the wall and patted the saddle gently, as if stabling a horse.

After Adam had introduced himself and explained his presence, Constable Taplow said: 'I suppose you'll be wanting to get on your way then. No point in hanging around. I'll deal with this.'

Adam said firmly: 'I'll come up with you. I've got the key. I thought it a prudent precaution to lock the door.'

Constable Taplow took the key and seemed about to comment on the over-fussiness of the Met, but refrained. They went up together. Taplow regarded the body with mild disapproval, surveyed the contents of the table, sniffed at the jar of ointment and took up the note.

'Seems plain enough to me. He couldn't face another family Christmas.'

'You've met the family before?'

'Never set eyes on any of them, except for the deceased. It's known that the family come to the hall every year but they don't show their faces, no more than he ever does – that is, did.'

Adam suggested mildly: 'A suspicious death, wouldn't you say?'

'No, I wouldn't, and I'll tell you why. This is where local knowledge counts. The family are all mad, or as near mad as makes no odds. His father did just the same.'

'Killed himself at Christmas?'

'Guy Fawkes Night. Filled all his pockets with Catherine wheels and bangers, stuffed bloody great rockets round his belt, drank a whole bottle of whisky and ran straight into the bonfire.'

'And went out with a bang, not a whimper. I hope there weren't any children present.'

'He went out with a bang, that's for sure. And they don't invite children to Harkerville Hall. You won't find Vicar bringing the carol singers round here tonight.'

Adam felt that he had a duty to persevere. He said: 'His desk is almost empty. Someone's been burning papers. The two half-burnt scraps are interesting.'

'Suicides usually burn papers. I'll look at them in good time. The paper that counts is here. This is a suicide note by any reckoning. Thanks for waiting, Sarge. I'll take over now.'

But when they reached the hall Constable Taplow said, with an attempt at nonchalance: 'Perhaps you'd drop me at the nearest telephone box. Better let CID have a look at this lot before they take the old gentleman away.'

Adam finally turned the MG seaward in the comfortable assurance that he had done as much as duty and inclination had required. If the local CID wanted him, then they knew where to find him. The Curious Case of the Christmas Cracker – an appropriate title, he felt, for such a bizarre preliminary to Christmas – could safely be left to the Suffolk police.

But if he had hoped for a peaceful evening, he was to be disappointed. He only had time to take a leisurely bath, unpack his case and settle himself before the driftwood fire with the first drink of the evening in his hand, when Inspector Peck knocked on the door. He was very different from Constable Taplow; young for his rank, with a sharp-featured expressive face under the dark hair, and apparently impervious to cold since he wore only slacks and jacket, his only concession to the December night a large multicoloured knitted scarf wound twice round his neck. He was gracefully apologetic to Miss Dalgliesh but wasted no such niceties on her nephew.

'I've done a bit of checking up on you, Sergeant. Not easy on Christmas Eve, but someone at the Met was alive and sober. Apparently you're the Inspector's blue-eyed boy. They say you've got a brain between your ears and eyes in your head. You're coming back with me to Harkerville Hall.'

'Now, Sir?' Adam's glance at the fire was eloquent.

'Now, as at this moment, at once, immediately, pronto. Bring your car. I'd drive you there and bring you back, but I've a feeling I'm likely to be at the hall for some little time.'

Night had fallen now. As Dalgliesh went to his car the air felt and smelt colder. The snow had finally ceased drifting down and a moon was reeling between the scudding clouds. At the hall they parked their cars side by side.

The door of the hall was opened by Mrs Dagworth who, with one malevolent look, let them in silently, then disappeared towards the kitchen. As they mounted the stairs Harkerville appeared.

Looking up at them, he said querulously: 'I thought you were going to have Uncle taken away, Inspector. It's hardly decent to leave him in his present state. Surely the district nurse can come and lay him out? This is all extremely upsetting for my sister.'

'All in good time, Sir. I'm waiting for the police surgeon and the photographer.'

'Photographer? Why on earth should you want him photographed? I consider that positively indecent. I've half a mind to telephone the Chief Constable.'

'You do that, Sir. I think you'll find he's with his son, daughter-in-law and grandchildren in Scotland, but I expect he'll be glad to hear from you. It'll quite make his Christmas, I don't wonder.'

In the bedroom Inspector Peck said: 'I suppose you're going to tell me that the suicide note isn't entirely convincing. I'm inclined to agree, but tell that to the coroner. You've heard the family history?'

'Some of it. I've heard about the ascension of grandfather.'

'And he wasn't the only one. The Harkervilles have an aversion to natural death. Their lives are unremarkable so they ensure that their deaths are spectacular. So what struck you particularly about this little charade?'

Dalgliesh said: 'A number of oddities, Sir. If this were a detective story, you could call it "The Twelve Clues of Christmas". It's taken a little mental agility to get the number to twelve, but I thought it appropriate.'

'Cut out the cleverness, laddie, and get to the facts.'

'This supposed suicide note for a start. It reads to me like the last page of a letter to one or more of the family. The paper was originally folded twice to get it into the envelope. The back is slightly singed. Someone has tried to iron out the creases. It hasn't been entirely successful; you can still see two faint marks. And then there's the wording. This was to be Harkerville's last Christmas. It suggests that he expected to suffer Gertrude's cooking for the final time, so why kill himself on Christmas Eve?'

'Changed his mind. Not unknown. What do you suggest the note means?'

'That he was planning to get away from here, perhaps to go abroad. There's a small segment of cardboard in the grate, with part of the head of a unicorn. You can just see the horn. I think someone burnt his passport, perhaps to conceal the fact that he's recently renewed it. There must have been travel documents, too, but the family burnt those together with most of his papers. And there's this scrap of half-burnt letter. It could be taken as a demand for money, but I don't think it is.

Look at the comma, Sir. There could have been other digits before the eight hundred pounds. For example, suppose it read 'four hundred thousand, eight hundred pounds not unreasonable considering the amount of land'. It could have been from an estate agent. Perhaps he was planning to sell up, add the proceeds to his existing fortune and say goodbye to this place for ever.'

'Escaping to the sun? Could be. And his darling will be waiting for him?'

'So she may be, but on the Costa Brava, not in Heaven. You should take a look next door at the maid's room, Sir. Nothing of any value left in the wardrobe and a pile of old clothes dumped unceremoniously in the waste-paper basket. Mavis is probably even now sitting in the sun waiting for a call from the aged person of her heart, dreaming of a few years of pampered luxury together, and then the rest of her life as a wealthy widow. Perhaps that's why he bothered with the hair restorer. It's rather pathetic, really.'

'You'll never make Inspector, lad, if you don't curb that imagination. As for the lass, she lives in the village. Easy enough to check whether she's at home.'

Adam said: 'Three clues so far: the singed note, the half-burnt passport, the scrap of letter. And then there's the ointment. Why bother with hair restorer if you're planning suicide?'

'Could be habit. Suicides don't always act rationally.

Well, the act itself is totally irrational. Why take the one option that cuts out all the other options? Still, I grant that plastering on that ointment was odd.'

'And he plastered it on thickly, Sir. Clue number four, the stained pillow. Rigor was just beginning to set in when I first saw him but I lifted the head. The pillow is sticky with the stuff, much more so than the paper hat. The hat must have been put on after he was dead. Then there's the cracker. If that was pulled here in the bedroom, where's the toy? The motto's in the cracker still but not the favour.'

Inspector Peck said: 'You're not the only one to search. I asked the family to leave the kitchen for a while and sit in the drawing room. I found this under the dresser.' He put his hand in his pocket and took out a sealed plastic envelope. Inside was a cheap gaudy brooch. He said: 'We'll check with the manufacturers but I don't think there's much doubt where this came from. God knows why they didn't pull the cracker in the bedroom, but some people are superstitious about making a noise in the presence of the dead. I'll grant you the Clue of the Christmas Cracker, Sergeant.'

'And what about the Clue of the Counterfeit Cook, Sir? Why would Harkerville instruct his nephew to advertise for one? He's known to be mean, a miser, and the note makes it plain that it was usually Gertrude who cooked the indigestible Christmas dinners. I think Mrs

Dagworth was brought in, not last night but this morning, to provide that evidence about hearing the cracker pulled just after nine o'clock and to give the others an alibi. If she arrived with them last night, as they claim, why is her case lying unopened on her bed next door? And she stated that the note was in Harkerville's handwriting. How did she know? It was Helmut Harkerville who claims he engaged her, not his uncle. And there's another thing: you've seen what a mess that kitchen is in. When she made tea for us and got out the old biscuits she knew exactly where to find what she wanted. She's worked in that kitchen before.'

'When do you suggest she arrived?'

'On this morning's early bus. It was important, after all, that Cuthbert Harkerville never saw her. She must have been here before. I think the family met her at Saxmundham. The car may be out of commission now, but when I arrived I saw two sets of tyre marks quite plainly in my headlights. They're obliterated by the snow now, but they were plain then.'

'Pity you didn't preserve them. They're not much good as evidence now. Still, you didn't know at the time there was anything suspicious about the death. I'll give you two clues for the counterfeit cook. A bit risky, though, wasn't it, putting themselves in the power of a stranger? Why not keep it in the family?'

'I think they did keep it in the family. If you call Mrs

Dagworth Mrs Helmut Harkerville, I think you might get a reaction. No wonder she's so sour, waiting on the others isn't exactly congenial.'

'Well, go on, Sergeant. We're not up to number twelve yet.'

'There's the holly, Sir. The stem is extremely prickly. There's no holly in this room, so someone must have brought it up, probably from the hall. If it were Cuthbert Harkerville, how did he manage to avoid pricking his fingers either when he carried it or when he pushed it through the buttonhole? And the stem of the holly isn't sticky with ointment.'

'He could have put the holly in place before he smeared that stuff over his scalp.'

'But would it have stayed in place? It's very loose in the buttonhole. I think it was put there after he was dead. It might be worth asking the counterfeit cook why her finger has a plaster. One point for the holly, Sir?'

'Fair enough, I suppose. I agree it must have been sticky if he'd stuck it in the buttonhole after he'd applied the ointment. All right, Sergeant, I know what you're going to say next. We're not exactly daft in the Suffolk CID. I suppose you're going to call it the Clue of the Christmas Pudding?'

'It does seem appropriate, Sir. It's obvious from examining the pudding – an unseasonably pale concoction I thought – that a piece has been gouged out of the top, not sliced. Someone stuck in a hand. If that hand was Cuthbert Harkerville's, why isn't there pudding under his nails? The only splodge of pudding is in his right palm. Someone smeared the palm after his death. It was a stupid error, but then the Harkervilles strike me as more ingenious than intelligent. I'm not sure that the final clue isn't the strongest. Judging by the onset of rigor, he probably died between eight and nine, early anyway. I think the family put an overdose of his sleeping pills into the thermos of strong coffee knowing that they'd be fatal taken with a generous slug of whisky. So why were the ashes in the grate still warm when I examined the fire eight hours later? And, more important, where are the matches? And that, by my reckoning, brings the number up to a seasonal dozen.'

'I'll take your word for it, Sergeant. God knows how I got drawn into this arithmetical nonsense. We've got a dozen questions. Let's see if we can get any answers.'

The Harkervilles were in the kitchen sitting disconsolately round the large central table. The cook was sitting with them but, as if anxious to show that this familiarity was unusual, almost sprang to her feet at their entrance. The wait had had its effect on the family. Adam saw that he and Inspector Peck were now facing three frightened people. Only Helmut attempted to hide his anxiety with bluster.

'It's time you explained yourself, Inspector. I demand that my uncle's body be decently laid out and removed and the family left in peace.'

Without replying, Peck looked at the cook. 'You seem curiously familiar with the kitchen, Mrs Dagworth. And perhaps you can explain why, if you arrived last night, your suitcase is still lying packed on your bed, and how you knew that the suicide note was in the deceased's handwriting?'

The questions, although mildly put, were more dramatic in their effect than Adam could have expected. Gertrude turned on the cook and screamed: 'You stupid bitch! Can't you do even the simplest thing without making a mess of it? It's been the same ever since you married into this family.'

Helmut Harkerville, trying to retrieve the situation said loudly: 'Stop it. No one is to answer any more questions. I demand to see my solicitor.'

'That, of course, is your right', said Inspector Peck. 'In the mean time, perhaps the three of you would be good enough to come with me to the station.'

Amid the ensuing expostulations, accusations and counter-accusations, Adam murmured a brief goodbye to the Inspector and left them to it. He pulled back the car hood and drove in a rush of cold cleansing air towards the growing rhythmic moaning of the North Sea.

Miss Dalgliesh had no objection to her nephew's job, thinking it entirely proper that murderers should be caught, but on the whole she preferred to take no active interest in the process. This evening, however, curiosity overcame her. While Adam was helping to carry the boeuf bourguignon and winter salad to the table, she said: 'I hope your evening wasn't interrupted for nothing. Is the case concluded? What did you think of it?'

'What did I think of it?' Adam paused for a moment and considered. 'My dear Aunt Jane, I don't think I'll ever have another case like it. It was pure Agatha Christie.'